WHEN LIGHTNING STRIKES TWICE

Originally published as "Ravensdene Court"

JOSEPH SMITH FLETCHER

A ccording to an entry in my book of engagements, I left London for Ravensdene Court on March 8th, 1912. Until about a fortnight earlier, I had never heard of the place, but there was nothing remarkable in my ignorance of it, seeing that it stands on a remote part of the Northumbrian coast, at least three hundred miles from my usual haunts. But then, towards the end of February, I received the following letter which I may as well print in full, for it serves as a fitting introduction to a series of adventures so extraordinary, mysterious, and fraught with danger, that I am still wondering how I ever came safely through them.

Dear Sir,

I am told by my friend Mr. Gervase Witherby, with whom I understand you to be well acquainted, that you are one of our leading experts in matters relating to old books, documents, and the like. The very man to inspect, value, and generally criticize the contents of an ancient library. Accordingly, I should be very glad to secure your valuable services. I have recently entered into possession of this place, a very old manor-house on the Northumbrian coast, wherein the senior branch of my family has been settled for some four hundred years.

There are here many thousands of volumes, the majority of considerable age. Also a large collections of pamphlets, manuscripts, and broadsheets compiled my uncle, and immediate predecessor, John Christopher Raven, who was renowned as a great collector in his day. However, from what I have seen of his collection up to now, I cannot say that he was a great exponent of the art of order, or a devotee of system, for an entire wing on this house is neither more nor less than a museum into which books, papers, antiques, and similar things appear to have been dumped without regard to classification or arrangement. As for myself, I am neither a bookman, nor an antiquary. My life until recently has been spent in far different fashion, as a Financial Commissioner in India. I am, however, sincerely anxious that these new possessions of mine should be properly cared for. I should therefore like an expert to examine everything that is here, and to advise me as to proper arrangement and provision for the future.

I should accordingly be greatly obliged to you if you could come here as my guest, give me the benefit of your expert knowledge, and charge me whatever fee seems good to you. I cannot promise you anything very lively in the way of amusement in your hours of relaxation, for this is a lonely place, and my family consists of nothing but myself and my niece, a girl of nineteen, just released from the schoolroom. That said, you may find some more congenial society in another guest of mine, Mr. Septimus Cazalette, the eminent authority on numismatics, who is here for the purpose of examining the vast collection of coins and medals formed by the kinsman I have just referred to.

I can also promise you the advantages of a particularly bracing climate, and assure you of a warm welcome and every possible provision for your comfort. In the hope that you will be able to come to me at an early date,

I am, dear sir,
Yours truly,
FRANCIS RAVEN.

. . .

Several matters referred to in this letter inclined me towards going to Ravensdene Court—the old family mansion, the thousands of ancient volumes, the prospect of unearthing something of great interest—and perhaps, more than anything else, the genuinely courteous and polite tone of my invitation. I was not particularly busy at that time, nor had I been out of London for more than a few days in several years: for which reason a visit to the far-flung North had its attractions. And so, after a brief correspondence with him, I arranged to visit Mr. Raven early in March, and remain under his roof until I had completed the task which he desired me to undertake.

As I have said already, I left London on the 8th of March, journeying to Newcastle by the afternoon express from King's Cross. I spent that night in the Northern metropolis and went forward next morning to Alnmouth, which according to my map was the nearest station to Ravensdene Court. And soon after arriving at Alnmouth the first chapter of my adventures opened, and came about by sheer luck.

It was a particularly fine, bright, sharply-bracing morning, and as I was under no particular obligation to present myself at Ravensdene Court at any fixed time, I determined to walk thither by way of the coast. The distance, according to my map, was about nine or ten miles. Accordingly, sending on my luggage by a conveyance, with a message to Mr. Raven that I should arrive during the afternoon, I made through the village of Lesbury toward the sea, and before long came in sight of it. A glorious stretch of blue, smooth as an island lake, and shining like polished steel in the light of the sun. There was not a sail in sight, north or south or due east, nor a wisp of trailing smoke from any passing steamer. I got an impression of silent, unbroken immensity which seemed a fitting prelude to the solitudes into which my mission had brought me.

I was at that time just thirty years of age, and though I had been closely kept to London of late years, my youth had been spent in lonely places, and I had an innate love of solitudes and wide spaces. I saw at once that I should fall in love with this Northumbrian coast, and once on its headlands I took my time, sauntering along at my leisure. Mr. Raven, in one of his letters, had mentioned seven as his dinner hour: therefore, I had the whole day before me. By noon the sun had grown warm, even summer-like; warm enough, at any rate, to warrant me in sitting down on a ledge of the cliffs while I smoked a pipe of tobacco and stared lazily at the mighty stretch of water across which, once upon a time, the vikings had swarmed from Norway. I must have become absorbed in my meditations—certainly it was with a start of surprise that I suddenly realized that somebody was near me, and looked up to see a man standing close and eyeing me furtively,

It was, perhaps, the utter loneliness of my immediate surroundings that made me wonder to see any living thing so near. At that point there was neither a sail on the sea, nor a human habitation on the land; there was not even a sheep cropping the herbage of the headlands. I think there were birds calling about the pinnacles of the cliffs—yet it seemed to me that the man broke a complete stillness when he spoke, as he quietly wished me a good morning.

The sound of his voice startled me, bringing me out of my reverie and sharpening my wits as I took him in from head to foot. A thick-set middle-aged man, he was tidily dressed in a blue serge suit of nautical cut, the sort of thing that they sell ready-made in sea-ports and naval stations. His clothes went with his dark skin and grizzled hair and beard, and with the gold rings which he wore in his ears.

"A fine morning," I remarked, not at all averse to entering into conversation, and already somewhat curious about him.

"A fine morning it is, master, and good weather, and likely to keep so," he answered, glancing around at sea and sky. Then he looked significantly at my knickerbockers and at a small satchel which I carried over my shoulders. "The right sort o' weather," he added, "for gentlemen walking about the country —pleasuring."

"You know these parts well?" I asked.

"No!" he said, with a decisive shake of his head. "I don't, master, and that's a fact. I'm from the south, I am—never been up this way before, and, queerly enough, for I've seen most of the world in my time, never sailed this here sea as lies before us. But I've a sort of connection with this bit of country—my mother's side came from hereabouts. And so, having nothing particular to do, I came down here to take a cast round, like, seeing places as I've heard of but never seen before."

"Then you're stopping in the neighbourhood?" I asked.

He raised one of his brown, hairy hands, and jerked a thumb landwards.

"Stopped last night in a little place inland," he answered. "Name of Lesbury—a riverside spot. But that ain't what I want —what I want is a churchyard, or it might be two, or it might be three, where there's gravestones what bears a name. Only I don't know where that churchyard may be, except somewhere between Alnmouth one way and Brandnell Bay, t'other."

"I have a good map, if it's any use to you," I said. He took the map with a word of thanks, and after spreading it out, traced places with the end of his thick forefinger.

"Hereabouts we are, at this present, master," he said, "and here and there is, to be sure, villages—mostly inland. They'll have graveyards to 'em, no doubt—folks must be laid away somewhere. And in one of them graveyards there'll be a name, and if I see that name, I'll know where I am, and I can ask further, aiming to find out if any of that name is still flourishing hereabouts. But till I get that name, I'm clear off my course, so to speak."

"What is the name?" I asked him.

"Netherfield," he answered, slowly. " My Mother's people— long since past as I've been led to understand. That's the name, right enough, only I don't know where to look for it. You ain't seen it, master, in your wanderings round these parts?"

"I've only come into these parts this morning," I replied. "But if you look closely at that map, you'll observe that there aren't many villages along the coast, so your search ought not to be a lengthy one."

"Aye, well, Netherfield is the name," he repeated. "And there may be some of 'em left—and then again there mightn't be. My own name being Quick—Salter Quick. Of Devonport—when on land, you see."

He folded up and handed back the map, with an old-fashioned bow. I rose from the ledge of rock on which I had been resting, and made to go forward.

"I hope you'll come across what you're seeking, Mr. Quick," I said. "But I should say you won't have much difficulty. There can't be many churchyards in this quarter, and not many gravestones in any of them."

"I found nothing in that one behind," he answered, jerking his thumb towards Lesbury. "And it's a long time since my mother left these parts. But here I am, anyway. Time's no object —nor yet expense. A man must take a bit of a holiday some day or other. Ain't had one myself for nigh on thirty years."

We walked forward, northing our course, along the headlands. Then, rounding a sharp corner, we suddenly came in sight of a little settlement that lay half-way down the cliff. There was a bit of a cottage or two, two or three boats drawn up on a strip of yellow sand, a crumbling smithie, and above these things, on a shelf of rock, a low-roofed, long-fronted inn. From its the gable rose a mast, from which a battered flag fluttered in the sea breeze. At the sight of this I saw a gleam come into my companion's eye, and I was quick to understand it's meaning.

"Do you feel disposed to a glass of ale?" I asked. "I should say we could get one down there."

"Rum," he replied, laconically. "Rum is my drink, master.

Used to that—I ain't used to ale. Cold stuff! Give me something that warms a man!"

"It's poor ale that won't warm a man's belly," I said with a laugh. "But every man to his taste. Come on, then."

He followed in silence down the path to the lonely inn. Once, looking back, I saw that he was turning a sharp eye round and about the new stretch of country that had just opened before us. From the inn and its surroundings a winding track wound off and upward into the land. In the distance I saw the tower of a church. Salter Quick saw it too, and nodded significantly in its direction.

"That'll be where I'll make next," he observed. "But first— meat and drink. I ate my breakfast before seven this morning, and this walking about on dry land makes a man hungry."

"Drink you'll get here, no doubt," said I. "But as to meat— that's doubtful."

His reply to that was to point to the sign above the inn door, to which we were now close. He read its announcement aloud, slowly.

"'The Mariner's Joy. Good Entertainment for Man and Beast,'" he pronounced. "'Entertainment'—that means eating— meat for man; hay for cattle. Not that there's much sign of either in these parts, I think, master."

We walked into the Mariner's Joy side by side, turning into a low-ceilinged, darkish room, neat and clean enough, wherein there was a table, chairs, the model of a ship in a glass case on the mantelpiece, and a small bar, furnished with bottles and glasses, behind which stood a tall, bespectacled middle-aged man reading a newspaper. He bade us good morning, with no sign of surprise at the presence of strangers, and looked expectantly from one to the other.

I turned to my companion. "Well?" I said. "You'll drink with me? What is it—rum?"

"Rum it is, master, thanking you," he replied. "But vittals, too, is what I want." He glanced knowingly at the landlord. "You

7

ain't got such a thing as a good plateful of cold beef, a loaf of home-baked bread, and a morsel of cheese to go with it?"

The landlord smiled as he reached for the rum bottle.

"I dare say we can fit you up, my lad," he answered. "Got a nice round of boiled beef on the go, as it happens. Drop of rum first, eh? And yours, sir?"

"A glass of ale if you please," said I. "And as I'm not quite as hungry as our friend here, a crust of bread and a piece of cheese."

The landlord satisfied our demands, and then vanished through a door at the back of his bar. When he had expressed his wishes for my good health, Salter Quick tasted the rum, smacked his lips over it, and looked about him with evident approval.

"Sort of port that a vessel might put into with security and comfort for a day or two," he observed closely. "I reckon I'll put myself up here, while I'm looking round—this will do me very well. And doubtless there'll be them coming in here, night-time, as'll know the neighbourhood, and be able to give a man points as to his bearings."

"I dare say you'll be very comfortable here," I assented. "It's not exactly a desert island."

"Aye well, Salter Quick's been in quarters of that sort in his time," he replied enigmatically, with a glance that suggested infinite meaning. "But this ain't no desert island, master. Not with good liquor in ready supply. I'll tell you that for nowt!"

He made his usual jerk of the thumb—this time in the direction of the landlord, who'd just returned with a well-filled tray. And presently, first removing his cap and saying his grace in a devout fashion, he sat down and began to eat with an evidently sharp-set appetite. Trifling with my bread and cheese, I turned to the landlord.

"This is a very lonely spot," I said. "I was surprised to see a licensed house here. Where do you get your customers?"

"Aye, you wouldn't see it as you came along," replied the

landlord. "But there's a village just behind here—by this head-land at the back of the house—that's a goodish-sized place. Plenty of custom from that on many a night. And of course, there's always folks going along, northwards and south."

Quick, his weather-stained cheeks bulging with food, looked up sharply.

"A village, says you!" he exclaimed. "Then if a village, a church. And if a church, I warrant a churchyard?"

"Just so," replied the landlord. "But what of it?"

Quick nodded at me.

"As I been explaining to this gentleman," he said, "church-yards is what I'm looking for. The graves in 'em, you understand. And on them graves, the name of Netherfield is what I seek. Now I ask you—have you ever seen that name in your church-yard? 'Cause if so I'll be dropping anchor."

"Can't say I have," answered the landlord. "But there might be that name on some of 'em, for aught I know—I've never looked 'em over. And our churchyard—Lord bless you—it's covered in tall grasses to be sure. That said . . ."

Just then there came into the parlour a man, who from his rough dress, appeared to be a cattle-drover or a shepherd. Claigue turned to him with a glance that seemed to indicate him as authority.

"Here's one as lives by that churchyard," he observed. "Jim, have you ever noticed the name of Netherfield on any o' them old gravestones up yonder? This gentleman's asking after it, and I know you mow that churchyard grass time and again."

"Never did!" answered the newcomer. "But it's funny you should mention it. There was a man come up to me the other night, this side o' Lesbury, and asked the very same question."

Before he could continue, Salter Quick dropped his knife and fork with a clatter, and held up his right hand with evident dismay.

❧ 2 ❧

It was clear to Claigue and myself, both interested spectators, that the newcomer's announcement, sudden and unexpected as it was, had prompted Quick to forget his beef and rum in an instant. Indeed, although he was only halfway through its contents, he pushed his plate away from him as if food were now nauseous. At the same time, he turned a startled eye on the speaker, looking him through and through as if in angry doubt of what had just been uttered.

"What's that?" he snapped. "What says you? Say it again—no, I'll say it for you—to make sure that my ears ain't deceiving me! You met a man—hereabouts—what asked you if you knew where there was graves with a certain name on 'em? And that name was Netherfield? Is that what you're telling me? Come on, man—spit it out!"

The drover, or shepherd, or whatever he was, looked from Quick to me and then to Claigue, and smiled, as if he wondered at Quick's intensity of manner.

"You've got it all right, mister," he answered. "That's just what I did say. A stranger, he was to boot—never seen him in these parts before."

Quick took up his glass and drank. There was no doubt about his being upset, for his big hand trembled.

"When was this?" he demanded.

"Two nights ago," replied the man readily. "I was coming home, lateish from Alnwick, and met with this here chap a bit this side o' Lesbury. We walked a piece of the road together, talking, and he asked me what I've told you. Did I know these parts? —was I a native hereabouts?—did I know any churchyards with the name Netherfield on gravestones? And I said I didn't, but that there was such-like places in our parts where you couldn't see the gravestones for the grass, and these might be what he was asking after. And when we came to them cross-roads, where it goes to Denwick one direction, and Boulmer the other, he left me, and I ain't seen aught of him since."

Quick pushed his empty glass across the table, with a sign to Claigue to refill it. At the same time he pointed silently to his informant, signifying that he was to be served at his expense. He was evidently deep in thought by that time, and for a moment or two he sat staring at the window and the blue sea beyond, abstracted and pondering. Suddenly he turned again on the drover.

"What did he look like, this stranger?" Quick persisted.

"I couldn't tell you, mister," replied the other. "It was well after dark and I never saw his face. But judging by the build of him, a strong-set man, like myself, and just about your height. And now I come to think of it, he spoke in your way—not as we do in these quarters. A seafaring man, I took him for."

"And you ain't heard of his being about?" asked Quick.

"Not a word, mister," affirmed the informant. "He went Denwick way when he left me. That's going inland."

Quick turned to me.

"I would like to see that map of yours again, master, if you please," he asked me. "I ought to have provided myself with one before I came here." After I'd handed it over, Quick spread the map out before him, and after taking another gulp of his rum, proceeded to trace roads and places with the point of his finger. "Denwick?" he muttered. "Aye I see that. And these places where there's a little cross?—that'll mean there's a church there?"

I nodded in the affirmative, silently watching him, and wondering what this desire on the part of two men to find the graves of the Netherfields might mean. The landlord evidently shared my wonder, for presently he phrased it directly: "You seem very anxious to find these Netherfield gravestones," he remarked, with good-humoured inquisitiveness. "And so, apparently, does another man. Now, I've been in these parts a good many years, and I've never heard of 'em; never even heard the name."

"Nor me!" said the other man. "There's none o' that name in these parts—'twixt Alnmouth Bay and Budle Point. I ain't never heard it!"

"And he's a native," declared the landlord. "Born and bred and brought up here. Isn't that right, Jim?"

"Never been away from it," assented Jim, with a short laugh. "Never been farther north than Belford, south than Warkworth, west than Whittingham. And as for east, I reckon you can't get much further that way than where we are already"

"Not unless you take to the water, you can't," said Claigue. "No—we ain't heard of no Netherfields hereabouts."

Quick seemed indifferent to these remarks. He suddenly folded up the map, returned it to me with a word of thanks, and then, plunging a hand in his trousers' pocket, produced a fistful of gold coins.

"Whatever's owed, take it out o' that," he asserted. "All we've had, and help yourself to a glass of something strong and a good cigar." Flinging a sovereign on the table, he rose to his feet. "I must be stepping along with this other fella abroad, seeking the——"

At that, he checked himself, remaining silent until Claigue counted out and handed over his change. Silently, Quick pocketed it and turned to the door. Claigue stopped him with an arresting word and motion of the hand.

"No business of mine, to be sure, but I wouldn't be brandishing that money of yours so readily hereabouts. There's folk up and down these roads that 'ud track you for miles on the chance of it—isn't that right, Jim?"

"Aye—and farther!" Jim assented. "You want to keep it tucked away."

Quick listened quietly—just as quietly he slipped a hand to his hip pocket and then brought out a revolver.

"This pistol and me are firm friends. I can swear to that," he said significantly. "Bad luck for anybody that comes between us and the light."

"They might come between you and the dark," retorted Claigue. "Take care of yourself! 'Tisn't a wise thing to flash a handful of gold about, my lad."

Quick made no remark. He walked out on to the cobbled pavement in front of the inn, and when I had paid Claigue for my modest lunch, and asked how far it was to Ravensdene Court, I followed him outside.

"Well?" I said, still inquisitive about his mysterious rival. "What next? Are you going on with your search?"

He scraped the point of a boot on the cobblestones for a while, gazing downwards, almost as if he expected to unearth something. Suddenly he raised his eyes again and gave me a franker look than I had so far seen from him.

"Master," he said in a low voice, and with a side glance at the open door of the inn, "I'll tell you a bit more than I've said before—you're a gentleman, I can see, and such as keeps his own counsel. I've a special reason for finding them graves. That's why I've travelled all this way—from one end of England to the other. And now, arriving where they ought to be, I find another man after the same thing. Nothing else explains his presence."

"Have you any idea who he may be?" I asked.

He hesitated, and then shook his head. "No, I haven't, and

that's a fact. For a minute or two, in there, I thought that maybe I did know, or, at any rate, had a notion. But that was nothing more than an idle fancy. All the same, I'm going Denwick way to see if I can come across whoever it is, or get news of him. Is that your road, master?"

"No," I replied. "I'm going some way farther along the headlands. Well—I hope you'll be successful in your search for the family gravestones."

He nodded, very seriously.

"I'm not going out o' this country till I've found 'em!" he asserted determinedly. "It's what I've come three hundred miles for, and I've never been one for turning back."

With a final sombre wave of farewell, he turned and took the dirt track that led over the top of the headlands. As long as I watched him, Quick went steadily forwards without even looking back, or to the right or left of him. Presently I, too, went on my way, rounding another corner of the cliff, where I left the lonely inn behind me. But as I went along, following the line of the headlands, I wondered a good deal about Salter Quick and the conversation at the Mariner's Joy.

What was it that this hard-bitten, travel-worn man was really after? I gave no credence to his story of the family relationship— it was not at all likely that a man would travel all the way from Devonshire to Northumberland to find the graves of his mother's ancestors. There was something beyond that, as he had himself acknowledged, without divulging the truth of the matter. But the nature of it eluded me. It was impossible to say. What deepened the mystery was the fact that two men—seafarers, both—had arrived in this out-of-the-way spot about the same time, unknown to each other, but apparently bent on the same object. It begged the question of what would happen if, as seemed likely, the two were to meet?

❦ 3 ❦

The afternoon remained fine, and, for the time of year, warm, and I took advantage of it by dawdling along that glorious stretch of sea-coast, taking in to the full its rich store of romantic scenery and hints of long-past ages. Sometimes I sat for a long time, smoking my pipe on the edge of the headlands, staring at the blue of the water, and the curl of the waves on the brown sands, only dimly aware of the calling of the sea-birds on the cliffs.

At length, the afternoon was drawing to its close when, rounding a bluff, I came in sight of what I felt sure to be Ravensdene Court. It was a grey-walled, stone-roofed Tudor mansion that stood at the head of a narrow valley through which a rock-encumbered stream ran murmuring to the sea. Very picturesque it looked in the mellowing light; the very place, I thought, where a collector of literary treasures might think to store them away.

A path led inland from the edge of the cliffs, and, after a few minutes' walking, I arrived at a rustic gate which was set in the boundary wall of a small park. Beyond the wall rose a belt of trees, mostly oak and beech, their trunks obscured by thick undergrowth. Passing through, I came out on the park itself, at a point where, on a well-kept green, a young woman was studying the lie of a golf ball. This I immediately took to be Mr. Raven's niece, of whom he had spoken in his letter, Behind her, carrying her bag of sticks, stood a small boy, chiefly remarkable for his large boots and huge tam-o'-shanter bonnet. As I appeared on the scene, he was intently watching his young mistress's putter, wavering uncertainly in her slender hands before she ventured on what was evidently a critical stroke. But before the stroke was made, the girl caught sight of me, paused, seemed to remember something, and then, swinging her club, came lightly in my direction.

She was a tallish, elastic-limbed girl, not exactly pretty, but full of attraction because of her clear eyes, healthy skin, and general atmosphere of life and vivacity. Although recently released from the schoolroom, she showed neither embarrassment nor shyness on meeting a stranger. Her hand went out to me with ready frankness.

"Mr. Middlebrook?" she said inquiringly. "Yes, of course—I might have known you'd come along the cliffs. Your luggage came this morning, and we got your message. But you must be tired after your long trek? I'll take you up to the house and give you some tea."

"I'm not at all tired, thank you," I answered. "I came along very leisurely, enjoying the walk. Don't let me take you from your game."

"Oh, that's all right," she said carelessly, throwing her putter to the boy. "I've had quite enough. Besides, it's getting towards dusk, and once the sun sets, it's soon dark in these regions. You've never seen Ravensdene Court before?"

"Never," I replied, glancing at the house, which stood some two or three hundred yards before us. "It seems to be a picturesque old place, romantically-situated. I suppose you know all its nooks and corners?"

She gave her shoulders a little shrug, and shook her head emphatically. "No. I had not seen it until last month, although I can find no fault with your first appraisal. Picturesque and romantic, it certainly is. And according to several legends, haunted as well."

"That adds to its charm," I remarked with a laugh. "I hope I shall have the pleasure of seeing one of these spectres."

"I don't!" she exclaimed good-naturedly. "That is, I hope I shan't. The house is strange enough without ghoulish denizens. There's a very odd atmosphere about the place. I'm not a coward, but, really, after the daylight's gone, it can be a little overwhelming."

"You're adding to its charms!" I replied. "It all sounds very Gothic. Exactly as I'd hoped before I set out here."

She looked at me inquiringly, and then smiled a little. "You're not at all as I'd thought you'd be."

"What were you expecting?" I asked, amused at her candour.

"Oh, I don't know—a queer, stuffy, fellow with a bald head like our Mr. Cazalette," she replied. "Bookish, and papery, and over the hill. Not a man in the first flush of youth."

"The frost of thirty winters have settled on me," I remarked with mock seriousness, rejecting her kind appraisal.

"They must have been black frosts, then!" she retorted. "No! —you're a surprise. I'm sure Uncle Francis is expecting a venerable, dry-as-dust sort of man."

"I hope he won't be disappointed," I said. "But I never told him I was dry as dust, or stuffy or bald for that matter."

"It's your reputation," she said quickly. "People don't expect to find such learning in ordinary young men in tweed suits."

"Am I an ordinary young man, then?"

"Oh, well, you know what I mean!" she said hastily. "You can call me an ordinary young woman, if it suits you."

"I shall do nothing of the sort!" said I. "I have a habit of always calling things by their right names, and I can see already that you are very far from being ordinary."

"So you begin by paying me compliments?" she retorted with a laugh. "Very well—I've no objection. But here is my uncle., striding towards us. Let's see what he has to say."

From the corner of my eye, I had already seen Mr. Francis Raven advancing to meet us. A tall, somewhat stooped man with a kindly face burnt brown by equatorial suns. Old-fashioned at first inspection, with grizzled moustache and whiskers—the sort of man that I had seen more than once coming off big liners at Tilbury and Southampton, looking as if England, seen again after many years of absence, were a strange country to their rather weary, wondering eyes. He came up with outstretched hands and I saw at once that he was a man of shy, nervous temperament.

"Welcome to Ravensdene Court, Mr. Middlebrook," he said in a quiet, almost deprecatory fashion. "A very dull and out-of-the-way place for one so used to London; but we'll do our best to entertain you." Turning to his niece, Mr. Raven smiled benevolently. "I see you've already received an advance welcome."

"As charming a one as her surroundings are delightful, Mr. Raven," I said, assuming an intentionally old-fashioned manner. "If I am treated with the same consideration during my stay, I shall be loath to bring my task to an end!"

"Mr. Middlebrook is a bit of a tease, Uncle Francis," said my guide. "I've found that out already. He's not the paper-and-parchment person you expected."

"Oh, dear me, I didn't expect anything of the sort!" protested Mr. Raven. He looked from his niece to me, and laughed, shaking his head. "These modern young ladies—ah!" he exclaimed. "But come—I'll show Mr. Middlebrook his rooms."

He led the way into the house and up the great stairs of the hall to a couple of apartments which overlooked the park. I had a general sense of big spaces, ancient heirlooms, mysterious nooks and corners. My own rooms, comprising of a bed-chamber and parlour, were perfectly delightful. Still, my host was painfully anxious to assure himself that I had everything that I was likely to want, and fussed about from one room to the other..

"You'll be able to find your way down?" he asked at last, as he made for the door finally. "We dine at seven—perhaps there'll be time to take a little look round before then, after we've dressed.

And I must introduce Mr. Cazalette—you don't know him personally? Oh, he's a remarkable man by any standards."

I did not waste much time preparing for dinner, nor apparently did Miss Marcia Raven, for I found her in the hall when I went down at half-past-six. She and I were still examining its multifarious objects when Mr. Raven appeared on the scene, followed by another man, who I took for Mr. Cazalette. One glance at this gentleman assured me that our host had been quite right when he spoke of him as remarkable. So extraordinary was he in outward appearance that I stared at him fixedly, despite the breach of social etiquette.

Miss Raven had already described Mr. Cazalette to me as a stuffy old man with a bald head, but that summary synopsis failed to do justice to the original. At first I thought this pronounced oddity derived from his clothes—for he wore a strangely-cut dress-coat of blue cloth, with gold buttons, a buff waistcoat, and a frilled shirt—but soon came to the conclusion that he would be uncommon in any garments. About Mr. Cazalette there was an atmosphere of decided mystery that was difficult to pin down to any one particular. First and last, he looked uncanny. A purveyor of Magick, or some such like.

Mr. Raven introduced us with a sort of old-world formality (I soon discovered that he was wholly unaware that a vast gulf lay between the manners and customs of society as they are nowadays and as they were when he left England for India in the 'seventies). In turn, I saluted Mr. Cazalette with great respect and expressed my pleasure at having met one so famous as my fellow-guest. Somewhat to my surprise, Mr. Cazalette's tightly-locked lips relaxed into what was plainly a humorous smile, and he favoured me with a knowing look that was almost a wink.

"Aye, well," he said, "you're just about as well known in your own line, Middlebrook, as I am in mine, and between the pair of us I've no doubt we'll be able to reduce chaos into order. But we'll not talk shop at this hour of the day—there's more welcome matters at hand."

He put his snuff box and his gaudy handkerchief out of sight, and looked at his host and hostess with another knowing glance, reminding me of a wicked old condor which I had sometimes seen at the Zoological Gardens, eyeing the keeper who approached with its meal.

"Mr. Cazalette," remarked Miss Raven, with an informing glance at me, "never touches bite or sup between breakfast and dinner."

"I'm a disciple of the justly famed and great man, Abernethy," explained Mr. Cazalette. "I'd never have lived to my age, nor kept my energy, if it hadn't been for the dietary regimen espoused by him . . .Do you know how old I am, Middlebrook?"

"I really don't, Mr. Cazalette," I replied.

"Well I'm eighty years of age," he answered with a grin. "And I'm intending to be a hundred! And on my hundredth birthday, I'll give a party, and I'll dance with the sprightliest lassie that's there, and if I'm not as lively as she is I'll be sore out of my calculations."

"A truly wonderful young man!" exclaimed Mr. Raven. "I veritably believe he feels—and is—younger than myself—and I'm twenty years his junior."

So I had now discovered certain facts about Mr. Cazalette. He was an uncannily active octogenarian with an almost imp-like desire to live—and to dance—when he ought to have been wrapped in blankets and saying his last prayers. And a few minutes later, when we were seated round our host's table, I discovered another fact—Mr. Cazalette was one of those men to whom dinner is the event of the day, and who regard conversation—on their own part, at any rate—as a wicked disturbance of sacred rites. As the meal progressed (and Mr. Raven's cook proved to be an unusually clever and good one) I was astonished at Mr. Cazalette's gastronomic powers and at his love of mad dishes. Indeed, I never saw a man eat so much, nor with such hearty appreciation of his food, nor in such concentrated silence.

Nevertheless, he kept his ears wide open to what was being

said around him, as I soon discovered. I was telling Mr. Raven and his niece of my adventure of the afternoon, when I suddenly observed that Mr. Cazalette had stopped eating—knife and fork still in his queer, claw-like hands—and was peering at me under the shaded lamps; his black, burning eyes full of a strange, absorbed interest.

I paused involuntarily on the other side of the table, somewhat unnerved by his fascination.

"Go on!" said he. "Did you mention the name Netherfield just then?"

I nodded in abeyance.

"Well, continue with your tale," he said. "I'm listening. I'm a silent man when I'm busy with my meat and drink, but I've a fine pair of ears for all that."

He began to ply knife and fork again as I went on with my story, until I reached the very end of it. By then, the footman in attendance was removing his empty plate, and the old man leaned back a little in his chair and favoured the three of us with an enigmatic gaze.

"Aye, well," he said, "that's an interesting story, Middlebrook, and it tempts me to break my cardinal rule and discourse at the dinner table. It was some churchyard this fellow was seeking, you say?"

"It certainly appeared so," I answered.

"Where there were graves with the name Netherfield on their stones or slabs or monuments?" Mr. Cazalette continued, seeking further clarification.

"Aye—just so. And yet those men at the inn had never heard of anything at that point, nor elsewhere."

"Then if there is such a place," said he, "it'll be one of those disused burial-grounds of which there are examples here in the north, and not a few of them."

"You know of some?" suggested Mr. Raven.

"I've seen such places," answered Mr. Cazalette. "Betwixt here and the Cheviots, heading westward, there's a good many spots that Goldsmith might have drawn upon for his deserted village. The folks leave, the local church falls into ruins, and its graveyard gets choked with weeds while the stones are covered with moss and lichen. In that way many an old family name now lies hidden. But why is that man seeking any name at all—that's what I'd like to know!"

"The curious thing to me," observed Mr. Raven, "is that two men should be wanting to find it at the exact same time."

"It looks as if there were some very good reason for it to be discovered?" observed Miss Raven. "Anyway, it all sounds very odd—you appear to have brought an intractable mystery with you, Mr. Middlebrook. Can't you suggest anything, Mr. Cazalette? I'm sure you're good at solving problems."

Just then, Mr. Cazalette's particular servant put a fresh dish in front of him—a curry, the peculiar aroma of which evidently aroused his epicurean instinct. Instead of responding to Miss Raven's invitation he relapsed into silence, and picked up another fork.

When dinner was over I excused myself from sitting with the two elder men over their wine—Mr. Cazalette turned out to have an old-fashioned taste for claret—and joined Miss Raven in the hall: a great, shadowy room with a great fire in its huge hearth-place, and deep, comfortable chairs set about it. In one of these I found her sitting, book in hand. She dropped it as I approached and pointed to a chair at her side.

"What do you think of that queer old man?" she asked in a low voice as I sat down. "Isn't there something almost—what is it?—uncanny?—about him?"

"You might call him that," I assented. "Indeed—uncanny fits him splendidly. A very marvellous man, though, at his age."

"Aye!" she exclaimed, under her breath. "If I could live to see it, it wouldn't surprise me if he lived to be four hundred. Do you know that he actually goes out early—very early—in the morning and swims in the open sea?"

"Any weather?" I asked.

"Rain or shine," she answered. "He's been here three weeks now, and has never once missed that morning swim of his."

"A most unusual character," I concurred again. "Although he does seem to fit in with his present surroundings. From what I have seen of it, Mr. Raven was quite right in telling me that this house was a museum."

I was looking about me as I spoke. The big, high-roofed hall, like every room I had so far seen, was filled from floor to ceiling with books, pictures, statuary, armour, curiosities of every sort and many ages. The prodigious numbers of books alone showed me that I had no light task in prospect. But Miss Raven shook her head.

"Museum!" she exclaimed. "You've seen nothing yet—wait till you encounter the north wing. I think my great-uncle, who left all this to Uncle Francis recently, must have done nothing except buy oddities of every description and then dump them down anywhere! At least there's a modicum of order here, but in the north wing, it's pure confusion."

"Did you know your great-uncle?" I asked.

"No," she shook her head. "I'd never been in the north until Uncle Francis came home from India some months ago and fetched me from the school where I'd been ever since my father and mother died. Except my father, I never knew any of the Raven family. I believe Uncle Francis and myself are the very last."

"You must like living under the old family roof?" I suggested.

She gave me an undecided look.

"I'm not quite sure. Uncle Francis is the very soul of kindness —I think he's the very kindest person, man or woman, I ever came across—but I still don't know if I really like this place. As I told you this afternoon, it's a very odd house altogether, and a strange atmosphere pervades it at all times. I have the distinct sensation that something must have happened here in days gone by."

"You'll get used to it," I remarked. "And I suppose there's always society."

"Uncle Francis is something of a recluse," she answered. "It's really a very good thing that I'm fond of outdoor life, and that I take an interest in books, although I can't lay claim to any deep knowledge. Do teach me something while you're here!—I'd like to know a great deal more about all these folios and quartos and so on."

I made haste to reply that I should be only too happy to put my knowledge at her disposal, and Miss Raven responded by saying that she would like to help me in classifying and inspecting the various volumes which the dead-and-gone great-uncle had collected. We got on very well together, and I was a little sorry when my host came in with his other guest, who proceeded to give us a learned dissertation on the evidences of Roman occupation of the North of England as evidenced by the recent discovery of coins between Trent and Tweed. It was doubtless very interesting, and striking proof of Mr. Cazalette's deep and profound knowledge of his special subject, and at another time I should have listened to it gladly. But somehow I should just then have preferred to chat quietly in the corner of the hearth with Miss Raven.

"We all retire early," Mr. Raven informed me with a shy laugh after the impromptu lecture had ended. "However, you will find a fire in my sitting-room, and if you wish to read or write then you should be comfortable in your retirement. "

"Actually, I'm in the habit of keeping regular habits and retiring to bed at ten o'clock. Reading and writing at night tend to stir the imagination and prompt insomnia."

Mr. Cazalette, stood to my right, nodded vigorously in approval. "Wise lad!" he said. "That's another reason why I am what I am. Don't let any mistake be made about it! Get to your pillow early, and leave it early—that's the sure thing to do!"

"I don't think I should like to get up as early as you do,

though," remarked Mr. Raven. "You certainly don't give the worms much chance!"

"Aye, and I've caught a few in my time," enthused the old gentleman. "And I hope to catch a few more before I'm finished. You folk who don't get up till the morning's half over don't know what you miss."

4

I slept soundly that night, unaffected by the strange bed and unfamiliar surroundings, and awoke feeling refreshed. My windows faced due east—I was instantly aware that the sun had either risen or was just about to rise. Springing out of bed, and drawing up one of the three tall blinds, I watched it emerge from behind a belt of pine and fir which stretched along a bluff of land that ran down to the open sea. And I saw, too, that it was high tide—the sea had stolen up the creek which ran right to the foot of the park, where the wide expanse of water glittered and sparkled.

My watch lay on the dressing-table close by. Glancing at it, I saw that the time was twenty-five minutes to seven. I had been told that the family breakfasted at nine, so I had nearly two-and-a-half hours of leisure before me, and therefore resolved to go outside and enjoy the freshness of the morning. I turned to the window again, just to take another view of the scenery in front of the house, and to decide in which direction I would go. There, I caught sight of Mr. Cazalette emerging from a wicket-gate that opened out of an adjacent field. It was evident that the robust octogenarian had been taking that morning swim of which Miss Raven had told me the previous evening. He was muffled up in an old pea-jacket, with various towels festooned about his shoulders, and his bald head catching the morning light.

I continued watching him as he came along the borders of a thick yew hedge at the side of the gardens. Suddenly, he stopped, removed something from his towels, then thrust it, using the full length of his arm, into the closely interwoven mass of twig and foliage.

Resuming his walk, as if nothing had happened, he moved towards the house again, disappearing behind a bushy clump of rhododendron. Two or three minutes later I heard a door close somewhere near my own; Mr. Cazalette had evidently re-entered his apartment.

My interest piqued, I was bathed, shaved, and dressed by a quarter past seven. Finding my way out of the house, I went across the garden towards the wicket-gate which Mr. Cazalette had passed through. My path led by the yew-hedge and I was able to see the place where he had stood when he thrust his arm into it. Thereabouts, the ground was soft and mossy, and the marks of his shoes were plain to see. Giving full reign to my curiosity, I parted the thick, clinging twigs and peeped into the obscurity behind it. There, thrust right in amongst the yew, I saw a crumpled lump of soiled white linen, looking very much like a man's full-sized pocket-handkerchief. Even in that obscurity I could discern brown stains and red stains, as if from contact with soil or clay in one case, and with blood in the other.

I went onward, considerably mystified, although at the same time I sought to rationalize the discovery. I came to the conclusion that Mr. Cazalette, during his morning swim, had cut hand or foot against some sharp pebble or bit of rock, and then used his handkerchief as a bandage until the bleeding stopped. Yet why thrust it away into the yew-hedge, close to the house? Why carry it from the shore at all, if he meant to get rid of it? Above all, why not consign it to his dirty-linen basket and have it washed thoroughly instead?

"Decidedly an odd character," I mused out loud. "A veritable man of mystery!"

Then I dismissed him from my thoughts, my mind becoming engrossed by the charm of my surroundings.

After making my way down to the creek, I passed through the belt of pine and fir over which I had seen the sun rise, and came out on a rock-bound cove that was desolate, wild, and dramatically situated. Here one was shut off from everything but the sea: Ravensdene Court was no longer visible amongst the great masses of fallen cliff and limpet-encrusted rock, round which the full strength of the tide was now washing.

I had not taken twenty paces along the foot of the over-hanging cliff before I pulled myself sharply to a halt. There, on the sand before me, lay Salter Quick—his face turned to the sky, his arms outstretched helplessly. And I knew, in that very first moment, that the poor man was dead.

5

My first feeling of abject horror at seeing a man whom I had met only the day before, struck down in the prime of life, soon changed to one of angry curiosity. Who had wrought this crime? For crime it undoubtedly was—the man's attitude, the trickle of blood from his slightly parted lips, the crimson stain on the sand at his side, the whole attitude of his helpless figure, showed me that he had been attacked from the rear and probably stricken by a deadly knife thrust through his shoulder blades.

This was murder—murder most foul. And my thoughts flew to what Claigue the landlord had said the previous afternoon about the foolishness of showing so much gold in public. Had Salter Quick disregarded that warning, flashing his money about in some other public house, and then been followed to this out of the way spot and run through the heart for the sake of his fistful of sovereigns? It looked like it. But then that thought fled, and another took its place—the recollection of the blood-stained linen which Mr. Cazalette had pushed into hiding in the yew-hedge. Had he himself played some part in the crime's commission?

The instinctive desire to get an answer to these questions

made me stoop down and lay my fingers on the dead man's right hand. It was stiff, rigid, stone-cold, suggesting that Salter Quick had been dead for several hours. In all likelihood, he'd been lying there, murdered, all through the darkness of the night.

There were no signs of any struggle. At this point the sands were unusually firm and for the most part, all round the body, they remained unbroken. Yet there were footprints, very faint indeed, yet traceable, and I saw at once that they did not extend beyond this spot. There were two distinct marks; one there of boots with nails in the heels—made by the dead man himself— while the other indicated a smaller, very light-soled boot; perhaps even a slipper. A yard or so behind the body these marks were mingled, which had evidently happened when the murderer stole close up to his victim, ready to deal the fatal thrust.

Carefully, I traced both sets of footsteps as best I was able. Faint though they were, I followed them to the edge of the low cliff, and a gentle slope of some twelve or fifteen feet. But from the very edge of the cliff the land was covered by a thick wire-like turf; you could have run a heavy gun over it without leaving any impression. Yet it was clear that two men had come across it to that point, had then descended the cliff to the sand, walked a few yards along the beach, and then—one had murdered the other.

Standing there, staring around me, I was startled by the sudden explosion of a gun in the immediate vicinity. And then, some thirty yards away, a man emerged from a coppice, whom I took to be a gamekeeper from his general appearance. Unconscious of my presence he walked forward in my direction, picked up a bird which his shot had brought down, and was thrusting it into a bag that hung at his hip when I called out to him.

He looked round sharply, caught sight of me, and came slowly in my direction with evident reluctance, as I elected to meet him halfway. He was a middle-aged man, big-framed, dark of skin and hair.

"Are you Mr. Raven's gamekeeper?" I asked as we came

within speaking distance. "I am staying with Mr. Raven, and I've just made the most terrible discovery. There is a man lying behind the cliff there—dead as can be."

"Washed up by the tide," he said, more as if stating a truth than advancing a speculation.

"No," I said. "He's been murdered. Stabbed to death!"

The man looked at me sceptically, as if I was guilty of pure fabrication.

"Come this way," I persisted, leading him to the edge of the cliff. "And see for yourself. But mind how you walk on the sand —there are footmarks here, and I don't want them interfered with till the police have examined them."

As we reached the edge of the turf, and came in view of the beach, he gave an exclamation of surprise, then followed me over to the dead man's side where he stood staring wonderingly.

"Did you see or hear anything of this man in the neighbourhood last night—or in the afternoon or evening?" I asked him.

"I, sir?" he exclaimed. "No, sir—nothing, I do solemnly swear!"

"I met him yesterday afternoon on the headlands between here and Alnmouth," I remarked.

"I was with him for a while at the Mariner's Joy. He pulled out a big handful of gold there to pay for his lunch. The landlord warned him against showing so much money. Now, before we do more, I'd like to know if he's been murdered for the sake of robbery. You're doubtless quicker of hand than I am—just slip your hand into that right-hand pocket of his and see if you feel money there."

He took my meaning on the instant, and bending down, did as I'd suggested. Moments later, he looked up in amazement and let out an astonished cry.

"Money?!" he said. "His pockets are bulging with it!"

"Very well then—bring it out."

Withdrawing his hand, he opened up his palm to reveal a dozen gold coins. The light of the morning sun flashed upon them as if in mockery. We both looked at the small treasure—and then at each other—with a sudden mutual intelligence.

"Then it wasn't robbery!" I exclaimed in perplexity.

With his free hand, my companion lifted a thick chain of steel which lay across Quick's waistcoat, bringing a fine watch into view.

"Gold again, sir!" he said. "And a good 'un, that's never been bought for less than thirty pound."

"No," I agreed, "and that makes this sordid business all the more mysterious. What's your name?"

"Tarver, sir," he answered, as he rose from the dead man's side. "At your service. Been on this estate many a year and never seen the like of it."

"Well, Tarver, I must go back to the house and tell Mr. Raven what's happened, and send for the police. In the meantime, I must ask you to stay here—and if anybody comes along, be very careful to keep them off those footmarks."

"Not likely that there'll be anybody about, sir," he remarked. "It's as lonely a bit of coast as there is here or hereabouts. What beats me is what he—and the man as did it—were doing on the beach to begin with?"

"The whole thing's a profound mystery," I answered, " and we shall no doubt hear a lot more of it."

Then I left him standing by the dead man and went hurriedly away towards Ravensdene Court. Glancing at my watch as I passed through the belt of pine, I saw that it was already getting on for nine o'clock and breakfast time. But this news of mine would have to be told: this was no time for standing on cere-mony. I must get Mr. Raven aside at once, and we must send for the nearest police officer.

Just then, fifty yards in front of me, I saw Mr. Cazalette vanishing round the corner of the long yew-hedge. So he had evidently been back to the place where he'd hidden the stained linen. Coming up to that place a moment later, and making sure that I was not observed, I looked in amongst the twigs and foliage. The handkerchief was now gone from there. This deepened the growing mystery more than ever. I began, against my will, to expand my conjectures.

Mr. Cazalette, returning from the beach, hides a blood-stained rag. I, going to the beach, find a murdered man. Coming back, I ascertain that Mr. Cazalette has already removed what he had previously hidden. What connection was there—if any at all—between Mr. Cazalette's actions and my discovery? To say the least of it, the whole thing was strange and downright suspicious.

Then I caught sight of Mr. Cazalette again. He was on the terrace, in front of the house, with Mr. Raven. The pair were strolling up and down before the open window of the morning room, both chatting volubly. I determined to tell my gruesome news straight out. Mr. Raven, I felt sure, was not a man to be startled by tidings of sudden death. Moreover, I wanted to see how his present companion would take the announcement.

❧ 6 ❧

After walking up the steps of the terrace, I called my host's name loudly. He turned, saw from my expression that something of moment had happened, and hastened toward me, with Cazalette trotting on behind him. I gave a warning look in in the direction of the house and its open windows.

"I don't want to alarm Miss Raven," I said in a low voice, which I purposely kept as matter-of-fact as possible. "You know the man I was telling you of last night—Salter Quick? Well I found his dead body on your beach, not half-an-hour ago. He has been murdered—stabbed to the heart by all appearances. Your gamekeeper, Tarver, is with the body now."

I carefully watched both men as I broke the news. Its effect upon them was different in both cases. Mr. Raven started a little, although he was more wonder-struck than horrified. However, Mr. Cazalette's mask-like countenance remained immobile; although I thought I spied a gleam of sudden interest—if not outright pleasure—in those shrewd blue eyes of his.

"Aye!" he exclaimed. "So you found your man dead and murdered, Middlebrook? Well, now, that's the very end that I was thinking the fellow would come to! Not that I fancied it would be so soon, nor so close at hand. Interesting! Very interesting!"

I was too much taken aback by his callousness to make any observation on these sentiments. Instead, I returned my attention to Mr. Raven. For his own part, he was too much surprised just then to pay any attention to his elder guest. Instead he motioned me to follow him.

"I must telephone the police," he said. "Of course, the poor fellow has been murdered for his money? You said he had a lot of gold on him?"

"It wasn't a robbery," I answered. "His money and watch were untouched. There's more in it than that."

He stared at me as if failing to comprehend.

"Some mystery?" he suggested.

"A very deep and lurid one, I think," said I. "Get the police out as quickly as possible, and bid them bring a doctor."

"They'll bring their own police surgeon," he remarked, "but we have a medical man closer at hand. I'll ring him up, too. Yet what can they hope to achieve with their examinations?"

"They may be able to tell us at what hour the murder took place, for one thing."

After Mr. Raven had made the call, we went into the morning-room to get a mouthful of food before going down to the beach. Miss Raven was there—so was Cazalette. I saw at once that he had told her the news. A cup of tea in one hand, a dry biscuit in the other, he was marching up and down the room, sipping and munching, and holding forth in didactic fashion on crime and detection.

Miss Raven was sat at the table, staring after him, but turned her attention to me as I took the neighbouring chair. "You found this poor man?" she whispered. "How dreadful for you!"

"For him, too—and far more so," I answered. "I didn't want you to know until later. Mr. Cazalette oughtn't to have told you."

She arched her eyebrows in the direction of the still orating figure.

"Oh!" she murmured. "He's no reverence for anything—life or death. I believe he's positively enjoying this. He's been carrying on like that ever since he came in and told me of it."

Mr. Raven and I made a very hurried breakfast and prepared to join Tarver. The news of the murder had spread through the household, and we found two or three of the men-servants ready to accompany us. Mr. Cazalette was ready, too, and more eager than any of them. Indeed, when we set out from the house, he led the way across the gardens and pleasure-grounds, and along the yew-hedge at which he never gave so much as a glance. At the further extremity of the pine wood. he glanced at Mr. Raven.

"From what Middlebrook says, this man must be lying in Kernwick Cove," he said. "Now, there's a footpath across the headlands and the field above from Long Houghton village to that very same spot. Quick must have followed it last night. But was it with the aim of meeting his murderer or did his nemesis follow him?"

Mr. Raven seemed to think these questions impossible of immediate answer. His one anxiety at that moment appeared to be to set the machinery of justice in motion. He was manifestly relieved when, as we came to the open country, where a narrow lane ran down to the sea, we heard the rattle of a light dog-cart and turned to see the inspector of police and a couple of his men in close attendance. They had evidently hurried here at once upon receiving the telephone message. With them, seated by the inspector on the front seat of the trap, was a professional-looking man who proved to be the police-surgeon.

Together, we all trooped down to the beach, where Tarver was keeping his unpleasant vigil. He had been taking a look round the immediate scene of the murder during my absence, thinking that he might find something in the way of a clue, but had turned up nothing of value. There were no signs of any struggle anywhere near to confirm that particular theory. All that could be safely said was that two men had crossed the land, descended the low cliffs, and that one had fallen on the other as soon as the sands were reached. I pointed out the relevant footprints to the police, who examined them carefully, and agreed with me that one set was undoubtedly made by the boots of the dead man, while the other belonged to a lightly-shoed person.

There being nothing else to be seen or done at that place, Salter Quick was lifted on to an improvised stretcher, which the servants had brought down from the Court, and carried by the way we had come to an outhouse in the gardens. There the police-surgeon proceeded to make a more careful examination of his body. He was presently joined in this by the medical man of whom Mr. Raven had spoken—a Dr. Lorrimore, who came hurrying up in his motor-car, and at once took a hand in his fellow-practitioner's investigations.

Just as I had thought from the first, Quick had been murdered by a knife-thrust from behind—dealt with evident knowledge of the right place to strike, said the two doctors. For his heart had been transfixed, and death must have been instantaneous.

Mr. Raven shrank away from these gruesome details, but Mr. Cazalette showed the keenest interest in them, and would not be kept from the doctor's elbows.

"And what sort of a weapon was it, d'ye suppose that the assassin used?" he asked. "That'll be an important thing to know."

"It might have been a seaman's knife," said the police-surgeon. "One of those with a long, sharp blade."

"Or," said Dr. Lorrimore, "a stiletto such as foreigners carry."

"Aye," remarked Mr. Cazalette, "or with an operating knife—such as you medicos carry with you! Any one of those fearsome things would serve to kill a man, undoubtedly."

The police inspector had by now got all of Quick's belongings in a little heap. They were, as I'd expected, highly considerable. Over thirty pounds in gold and silver., plus twenty pounds in notes in an old pocket-book. His gold watch, rich in detail, and certainly a valuable one. A pipe, a silver match-box, and a tobacco box, quaintly ornamented. Various other small matters, but, with one exception, no papers or letters. The one exception was a slightly torn, dirty envelope addressed in an ill-formed handwriting to Mr. Salter Quick, care of Mr. Noah Quick, The Admiral Parker, Haulaway Street, Devonport. There was no letter inside it, nor was there another scrap of writing anywhere about the dead man's pockets.

The police allowed Mr. Cazalette to inspect these things, according to his fancy. It was very clear to me by that time that the old gentleman had some taste for detective work. I watched him with curiosity while he examined Quick's money, his watch (of which he took particular notice, even going so far as to jot down its number and the name of its maker on his shirt cuff), and the rest of his belongings. But nothing seemed to excite his interest very deeply until he began to finger the tobacco box. Only then did his eyes widen as he turned to me excitedly.

"Middlebrook!" he whispered, edging me away from the others. "Look here, my lad! D'ye see the inside of the box lid? There's been something—a design, a plan, something of that sort —scratched into it with a knifepoint." Turning suddenly on the inspector, Mr. Cazalette sought instant confirmation. "What are you going to do with all these things?" he asked. "Take them away?"

"They'll all be carefully sealed up and locked up till the inquest, sir," replied the inspector. "No doubt the dead man's relatives will want to claim them."

Mr. Cazalette laid down the tobacco box, left the place, and hurried away in the direction of the house. Within a few minutes he came hurrying back, carrying a camera. He went up to the inspector with an almost wheedling air.

"Ye'll just indulge an old man's fancy?" he said, placatingly. "There's some queer markings inside the lid of the box that the poor man kept his tobacco in. I'd like to take a photograph of these if I may."

The police inspector, a somewhat stolid man, looked down from his superior height on Mr. Cazalette's eager face with a half-bored, half-tolerant expression. He had already seen a good deal of the old gentleman's fussiness.

"What is it about the box that demands such measures?" he inquired.

"Certain marks on it—inside the lid—warrant further study," answered Mr. Cazalette. "They're small and faint, but if I get a good negative of them, I can enlarge the image. And I say again, you don't know what one might find—any little detail is of value in a case of this sort."

The inspector picked up the metal tobacco box from where it lay amidst Quick's belongings and looked inside the lid. It was very plain that he saw nothing there except meaningless scratches. With an air of indifference, he put the thing into Mr. Cazalette's hands.

"I see no objection," he said. "Let's have it back when you've done with it, though. We shall have to exhibit these personal properties before the coroner."

Mr. Cazalette carried the tobacco box outside the shed in which the dead man's body lay, and busied himself with the camera. A gardener's potting-table stood against the wall. On this, backed by a black cloth which he had brought from the house, he set up the box and prepared to photograph it. It was evident that he attached great importance to what he was doing.

"I shall take two or three negatives of this, Middlebrook," he observed, consequentially. "I'm an expert in photography, and I've got an enlarging apparatus in my room. Before the day's out, I shall have something of note to show you."

Personally, I had seen no more in the inner lid of the tobacco box than the inspector—just a few lines and scratches—and so I left Mr. Cazalette to his self-imposed labours and rejoined the doctors and police. That Quick had been murdered there was no doubt; there would have to be an inquest, of course, and for that purpose his body removed to the nearest inn, a house on the crossroads just beyond Ravensdene Court. A search was to be set up at once for suspicious characters, and Noah Quick, of Devonport, contacted at the earliest opportunity.

All this the police took in hand, and I saw that Mr. Raven was heartily relieved when he heard that the dead man would be removed from his premises and that the inquest would not be held there. Ever since I had first broken the news to him, he had been upset and nervous. I could see that he was one of those men who dislike fuss and publicity. He threw me a commiserating look when the police questioned me closely about my knowledge of Salter Quick's movements on the previous day, and especially about his visit to the Mariner's Joy.

"Yet," said I, finishing my account of that episode, "it is very evident that the man was not murdered for the sake of robbery, seeing that his money and watch were found on him untouched."

The inspector shook his head.

"I'm not so sure," he remarked. "The man's clothes have been searched. You can see clear evidence . . .."

Turning to Quick's garments, which had been removed prior to interment, he picked up the waistcoat. Within the right side, there was a pocket, secured by a stout button. That pocket had been turned inside out. So, too, had a pocket in the left hip of the trousers, in which Quick had carried the revolver that he had shown me at the inn. The waistcoat's lining, as I could see now, had been ripped open by a knife in several places. And the lining of the man's hat had been torn out, too, and then thrust roughly into place again.

"It wasn't money they were after," observed the inspector, "but they must have been seeking an object of some implicit value. And the fact that the murderer has left all this gold untouched is the worst feature of the affair from our own point of view."

"How so?" inquired Mr. Raven.

"Because, sir, it shows that the murderer, whoever he was, had plenty of money about him," replied the inspector grimly. "And as he had, he'd have little difficulty in getting away. Probably he caught an early morning train, north or south, and is hundreds of miles off by this time. But we must do our best to catch him, all the same—and that's exactly what we'll do."

7

Leaving everything to the police—with obvious relief—Mr. Raven retired from the scene, inviting the two medical men and inspector into the house with him. To take, as he phrased it, "a little needful refreshment". At the same time he sent out a servant to minister to the constables in the same fashion.

Declining the invitation to join them, I turned into the big hall and there found Miss Raven. I was glad to find her alone. Indeed, the mere sight of her, in her morning freshness, was welcome after the gruesome business in which I had just been engaged. I think she saw something of my thoughts in my face, for she turned to me sympathetically.

"What an unfortunate thing that this should have happened at the very beginning of your visit," she said sombrely. "It must have given you an awful shock to find that poor fellow."

"It was certainly not a pleasant experience," I answered. "Although—strange as it is to say—I was not quite as surprised as you might think."

"Why not?" she asked.

"Even yesterday, it seemed to me that the man was running tremendous risks by showing his money in so cavalier a fashion.

And of course, when I found him, I thought he'd been murdered for his wealth."

"And yet he wasn't!" she said. "For you say it was all found on him. What an extraordinary mystery!"

"Indeed. A most extraordinary one. It seems impossible to fathom. But perhaps I would be better served focusing my energies on the task at hand, and for which my services have been enlisted. Would you be so good as to show me round the house, Miss Raven, so that I can learn what the extent of my labours are to be."

She at once acquiesced to this proposition, and we began to inspect the accumulations of the dead-and-gone master of Ravensdene Court. As his successor had remarked in his first letter, Mr. John Christopher Raven, though obviously a great collector, had certainly not been a great exponent of system and order. Except in the library itself, where all his most precious treasures were stored in tall, locked bookcases, his gatherings were lumped together anyhow and anywhere. The North wing, as Miss Raven had warned me, represented the apex of this chaos. The late Mr. Raven appeared to have bought books, pamphlets, and manuscripts by the cart-load, and it was very plain to me, as an expert, that the greater part of his possessions had never even been examined.

Before Miss Raven and I had spent an hour going from one room to another, I had arrived at two definite conclusions. One, that the dead man's collection of books and papers was about the most heterogeneous I had ever laid eyes on—containing much of great value and plenty of none whatsoever. The other, that it would take me a very long time to make a careful and proper examination of all its contents, and longer still to arrange it in proper order. Clearly, I should have to engage Mr. Raven in a business talk, and find out what his ideas were in regard to putting his huge library on a proper footing.

Mr. Raven at last joined us in one of the much-encumbered rooms. With him was the doctor Lorrimore, whom he had

mentioned to me as living near Ravensdene Court. He introduced the man to his niece, with, I thought, some evident signs
of pleasure.

"Dr. Lorrimore and I have been having quite a good talk.," he
said, glancing from me to Miss Raven, and then to the doctor
with a smile that was evidently designed to put us all on a
friendly footing, "It turns out that he has spent a long time in
India, so we have a lot in common."

"How very nice for you, Uncle Francis!" said Miss Raven. "I
know you've been bored to death with having no one you could
talk to about curries, brandy-pawnees, and such like. Were you
long in India, Dr. Lorrimore?" she asked.

"Twelve years," answered the doctor. "I came home just a
year ago."

"To bury yourself in these wilds!" remarked Miss Raven.
"Doesn't it seem quite out of the world here after that?"

Dr. Lorrimore smiled meaningfully at Mr. Raven, and showed
a set of very white teeth in doing so. He was a tall, good-looking
man, dark of eye and hair, moustached and bearded, but with the
faintest trace of silvery grey about his temples. A rather notable
man, I thought, who was evidently scrupulous about his appearance. Indeed, with his faultlessly cut frock suit of raven black,
glossy linen, and smart boots, he looked more fitted to a Harley
Street consulting-room than Northumbrian cottages and
farmsteads.

Now he transferred his somewhat mechanical smile to Miss
Raven.

"On the contrary," he said in a quiet tone, "this places suits
me to perfection. I bought the practice knowing it would not
make great demands on my time, allowing me to devote myself a
good deal to certain scientific pursuits in which I take a deep
interest."

"He has promised to put in some of his spare time with me
when he wants company," said Mr. Raven. "We have a great deal
in common."

"Dark secrets of a strange country!" remarked Dr. Lorrimore, with a sly glance at Miss Raven. Then, excusing himself from the offer of lunch, he took himself off.

Mr. Cazalette made no appearance at the table when the meal was convened. I heard a footman inform Miss Raven that he had just taken Mr. Cazalette's beef-tea to his room and that he required nothing else. I did not see him again until late that afternoon, when he suddenly appeared in the hall, where the rest of us were gathered by the tea-table before a cheery fire.

Taking his usual cup of tea and dry biscuit, he sat down in silence, although a smile of grim satisfaction played over his wizened features.

"Well, Mr. Cazalette," I said, succumbing to curiosity, "have you brought your photographic investigations to any successful conclusion?"

"Yes, Mr. Cazalette," chimed in Miss Raven, whom I had told of the old man's odd fancy about the scratches on the lid of the tobacco box. "We're dying to know if you've found anything out."

He gave us a knowing glance over the rim of his tea-cup.

"Aye!" he said. "But I'm not going to say what I've discovered, nor how far my investigations have gone. Ye must just die a bit more, Miss Raven, and maybe when ye're on the point of demise I'll resuscitate ye with the startling news of my great achievements."

I knew by that time that when Mr. Cazalette relapsed into his native Scotch, he was at his most serious, and that his bantering tone was assumed as a cloak. It was clear that we were not going to get anything out of him just then. But Mr. Raven tried another tack, fishing for information.

"You really think those marks were made of a purpose, Cazalette?" he suggested. "You think they were intentional?"

"I'll not say anything at present," answered Mr. Cazalette. "Except to remark that yon murderer was far from the ordinary."

Miss Raven shuddered a little.

"I hope the man who did it is not hanging about!" she said.

Mr. Cazalette shook his head with a knowing gesture.

"Ye need have no fear of that, lassie!" he remarked. "The man that did it had put a good many miles between himself and his victim long before Middlebrook there made his remarkable discovery."

"Isn't that guesswork?" I asked, feeling a bit restive under the old fellow's bluff confidence.

"No," said he, shaking his head firmly.. "It's deduction—and common-sense. Mine's a nature endowed with both admirable qualities, Middlebrook."

Shortly afterwards, as our group disbanded, I went off to continue some preliminary work that I had begun in the library. There, I began to think over the first events of the morning, and to wonder if I ought not to ask Mr. Cazalette for some explanation of the incident of the yew-hedge. He had certainly secreted a piece of blood-stained, mud-discoloured linen in that hedge for an hour or so. Why was he so secretive about it? Had it anything to do with the crime?

Had he picked it up on the beach when he went for his dip? And if so, and it was something of the moment, why had he not carried it straight to his own room in the house instead of hiding it? The circumstance was extraordinary, to say the least.

But on reflection I determined to hold my tongue and bide my time. For all I knew, Mr. Cazalette might have cut one of his feet on the sharp stones on the beach, used his handkerchief to staunch the wound, thrown it away into the hedge, and then, with a touch of native parsimony, have returned to recover the discarded article. At the same time, he was clearly interested in the murder of Salter Quick, and I had gathered from his behaviour and remarks that this sort of thing—investigation of crime—had a curious fascination for him. One thing was very sure, and the old man had grasped it readily—this crime was no ordinary one.

As twilight approached, making my work in the library impossible, and having no wish to go on with it by artificial light, I went out for a walk. The fascination which is invariably exercised on us by such affairs, led me back to the scene of the murder. The tide, which had been up in the morning, was now out, though just beginning to turn again. The beach, with its masses of bare rock and wide-spreading deposits of seaweed, looked bleak and desolate in the uncertain grey light.

But the scene was not without life—two men were standing near the place where I had come upon Salter Quick's dead body. Going nearer to them, I recognized one as Claigue, the landlord of the Mariner's Joy. He recognized me in turn, and touched his cap with a look that was alike knowing and confidential.

"So it came about as I'd warned him, sir!" he said, without preface. "I told him how it would be. You heard me! A man carrying gold about him like that—and showing it to all and sundry!"

"The gold was found on him," I answered. "And his watch and other things. He wasn't murdered for his property."

Claigue uttered a sharp exclamation. He was evidently taken aback.

"You hadn't heard that, then?" I asked.

"No," he replied. "I hadn't, sir. We've heard naught except that he was found murdered here, early this morning. Of course, I concluded that it had been for the sake of his money—that he'd been pulling it out in some public house or other and had been followed on account of it. Dear me, that puts a different complexion on things. Now, what's the meaning of it, in your opinion?"

"I have none," I answered. "The whole thing's a mystery. The doctors are of the opinion that he was murdered here around eight or nine o'clock last night, but that still begs the question: what was he doing at this lonely spot?"

The man who was with Claigue offered an explanation. There was, he said, a coast village or two further along the headlands; it would have been a short cut to reach them by end of day.

"Yes," said I, "but that would argue that he knew the lie of the land. Yet according to his own account, he was a complete stranger."

"Aye!" broke in Claigue. "But he must have fallen in with somebody, somewhere, that brought him down here and left him for dead."

Presently we parted. Claigue and his companion going back to the inn, and I to Ravensdene Court. The dusk had fallen by that time, and the house was lighted when I came back. Entering by the big hall, I saw Mr. Raven, Mr. Cazalette, and the police inspector standing in close conversation by the hearth. Mr. Raven beckoned me to approach.

"Here's some most extraordinary news from Devonport— where Quick hailed from," he said. "The inspector wired the police there this morning, telling them to communicate the news to his brother, whose name, as you know, was found on the dead man. He's had a wire back from them this afternoon."

At this, Mr Raven turned to the inspector, who placed in my hand the said telegram.

It read thus:

Noah Quick found murdered at a lonely spot on riverside near Saltash at an early hour this morning. So far no clue whatever as to his murderer.

❧ 8 ❧

I handed the telegram back to the police inspector with a glance that took in the faces of all three men. It was evident that they were thinking the same thought that had flashed into my own mind, although the inspector was first to give it voice:

"This," he said, tapping the bit of flimsy paper with his finger, "confirms the extraordinary nature of this whole intrigue. When two brothers are murdered on the same night, at places hundreds of miles apart, it signifies something uncommonly rare."

"It'll be at Devonport that the secret lies," observed Mr. Cazalette suddenly.

"Well, we're no closer to unearthing it this end, despite our best efforts," conceded the inspector. "We haven't come across a single person who saw this man after he left you yesterday afternoon, Mr. Middlebrook. My men have inquired in every village and at every farmstead and wayside cottage within an area of twelve miles, and are yet to hear word of him."

"Isn't it most likely that Quick came across the man of whom he'd heard at the Mariner's Joy?" I conjectured. "The man who, like himself, was asking for information about an old churchyard in which the Netherfields are buried."

"We've interviewed Jim Gelthwaite, the drover, but he was unable to elaborate on what he'd told you already. And nobody else seems to have seen that man, any more than they've seen Salter Quick."

"I suppose there are places along this coast where a man might hide?" I suggested.

"There may be," admitted the inspector. "Of course I shall have it searched thoroughly."

"Aye, but ye'll not find anything now," affirmed Mr. Cazalette. "The railway's not that far and there's early morning trains going north and south."

"We've questioned railway staff at the nearest stations," remarked the inspector. "And they could tell us nothing, either. It seems to me that Mr. Cazalette has hit the nail on the head in saying that Devonport will offer far more ready explanations. I'm coming to the conclusion that the whole affair was engineered from that quarter."

"Aye!" said Mr. Cazalette, laconically confident. "Ye'll learn more about Salter when ye hear more about Noah. It's a bonny mystery, all right, and with an uncommonly deep bottom to it. That much we do know for sure."

"I've wired to Devonport for full particulars," said the inspector. "No doubt I shall have them by the time our inquest opens tomorrow."

✥ 9 ✥

Next morning, Mr. Raven, Mr. Cazalette, the gamekeeper Tarver, and myself walked across the park to the wayside inn to which Salter Quick's body had been removed, and where the coroner was to hold his inquiry. However, nothing was revealed that day beyond what we knew already. Still, I was so much interested in the mystery that I carefully collected all the newspaper accounts concerning the murders at Saltash and Ravensdene Court, and pasted the clippings into a book for posterity. From these, I can now give something like a detailed account of all that was known of Salter and Noah Quick previous to the tragedies of that spring.

Somewhere about the end of 1910, Noah Quick became licensee of a small tavern called The Admiral Parker in a back street in Devonport, being in possession of plenty of cash, despite hailing from nowhere in particular. It was a fully-licensed establishment, much frequented by seamen. Noah Quick himself was a thick-set, sturdy middle-aged man, reserved and taciturn by nature, and very strict in his attention to business. He was a bachelor, keeping an elderly woman as housekeeper, a couple of stout women servants, a barmaid, and a potman. His house was particularly well-conducted and local police had never once had any complaint in reference to it.

Clearly, Noah was adept at keeping order, even when dealing with a rather rough class of customer. One witness, having watched him at work, had formed the opinion that he must have held some position of authority, and was accustomed to obedience, before going into the public-house business. Either way, everything seemed to be going very well with him and the Admiral Parker, when, in February 1912, his brother Salter made an appearance in Devonport.

Nobody knew anything about Salter Quick, except that he was believed to have come from Wapping or Rotherhithe, or somewhere about those Thames-side quarters. He was very like his brother in appearance, but far more sociable and talkative by nature. Having taken up residence at the Admiral Parker, he and Noah evidently got on together very well, and were affectionate in manner toward each other. They were often seen in company, but those who knew them best at this time noted that they never paid visits to, nor received visits from, any one coming within the category of friends or relations. One man, giving evidence at the inquest on Noah Quick, said that Salter, in a moment of confidence, had once told him that he and Noah were orphans, and hadn't a blood-relation in the world.

According to all that was brought out, matters went quite smoothly and pleasantly at the Admiral Parker until the 5th of March, 1912. Three days, it will be observed, before I myself left London for Ravensdene Court. On that date, Salter Quick cashed a check for sixty pounds. at a Plymouth bank, to which he'd been introduced by Noah. In the early afternoon, he went away, remarking to the barmaid at his brother's inn that he was first going to London and then farther north. Noah accompanied him to the railway station, where, as far as any one knew, Salter was not burdened by any luggage.

After he had gone, things went on just as usual at the Admiral Parker. Neither the housekeeper, nor the barmaid, nor the potman, could remember that the place was visited by any suspicious characters. Nor that its landlord otherwise showed any signs of notable distress. It was then, on the evening of March 9th (the very day on which I met Salter Quick on the Northumbrian coast), that Noah told his housekeeper and barmaid that he had to go over to Saltash to see a man on business, and should be back about closing-time. He went away about seven o'clock, but there was still no sign of him come midnight. None of his people heard any more of him until just after breakfast next morning. It was then that police came and told them that their employer's body had been found at a lonely spot on the bank of the river, a little above Saltash, and that he had been murdered for sure.

Clearly, there were points of similarity between the murders of the two brothers. The movements of each man were traceable up to a certain point, after which nothing of substance could be discovered. As regards Noah Quick, he had crossed the river between Keyham and Saltash by ferry boat, landing just beneath the great bridge that links Devon with Cornwall. It was nearly dark then, but he was seen and spoken to in passing by several men who knew him well. After that, he'd gone up the steep street towards the head of the old village, where he went into one of the inns and had a glass of whisky at the bar, exchanged a word or two with some men sitting in the parlour, and then went out again. Beyond that – as with his brother – Noah Quick's final movements were shrouded in mystery.

His dead body was found next morning at a lonely spot on an adjacent creek by a local fisherman. Like Salter, he had been stabbed; and in similar fashion. And as in Salter's case, robbery of money and valuables had not been the murderer's objective. Noah Quick, when found, was still wearing his gold watch and diamond ring, and had plenty of silver about him. His pockets had been turned out, the lining of his waistcoat slashed and slit, and his thick reefer jacket had been torn off and cut to pieces.

Close by lay his hard felt hat, whose lining had been torn out as well.

This, according to the evidence given at the inquests, and the facts collected by police, was all that could be safely ascertained. No one could say what became of Salter Quick after he left me outside the Mariner's Joy, just as no one knew where Noah Quick went when he walked out of the Saltash inn into the darkness. At each inquest, a verdict of wilful murder against some person or persons unknown was returned, and the respective coroners uttered vapid platitudes about coincidence and mystery. But from all that had transpired, it seemed to me that there were certain things to be deduced, and these I wrote down for my own meagre satisfaction:

1. Salter and Noah Quick were in possession of some secret.

2. They were murdered by men who wished to gain possession of it for themselves.

3. The actual murderers were probably two members of a gang.

4. If they had secured possession of the secret then they would surely make use of it.

As to the secret's nature, I was repeatedly drawn back to Mr. Cazalette and the yew-hedge affair. He never mentioned it—nor for some time, his tobacco box labours—but I was still loath to question him directly. However, as the two inquests drew to a close, I observed that he was spending what leisure he had in turning over old books which related to local history and topography. He was also studying maps and charts with the same regional purview, and had even ordered the latest Ordnance Map from London. Yet he made no mention of these things until one day, coming across me in the library, he suddenly let loose with a question.

"Middlebrook!" said he, "the name which that poor man mentioned to you as you talked with him on the cliff—am I right in thinking it was Netherfield?"

"That's correct," I answered. "What of it, Mr. Cazalette?"

He helped himself to a pinch of snuff, as if to assist his thoughts.

"Well, it's a queer thing that at the time of the inquest nobody ever thought of inquiring if there is a churchyard and such graves as the man sought so avidly."

"Why didn't you suggest it?" I asked.

"I'd rather find it out for myself," said he, with a twinkle in his eye. "Which is why I've looked through every last scrap of printed matter relating to this corner of the world that the late John Christopher Raven saw fit to collect; and still I can't find any reference to such a name."

"Have you tried the parish registers?" I suggested.

"Aye, I've consulted those as well, but with no more success."

"What about your photographic work on that tobacco box lid?" I asked. "Has that shone any light on the mystery?"

My question clearly caught him off guard. Untypically, the old man looked to the floor, avoiding my gaze, and answered evasively. "I couldn't say as yet. I'm still not through with that matter."

Later that day, I told Miss Raven of our little conversation. She and I were often together in the library, where we continued to discuss the mystery of the twin murders at length.

"What was there on the lid of the tobacco box?" she asked. "You saw it clearer than me. Anything that could actually arouse one's curiosity?"

"There were certainly some marks or scratches which seemed to have been made by design, but I think Mr. Cazalette exaggerated their importance," I replied.

"What precise significance did he attribute to them?"she asked again.

"That I couldn't say," I answered. "Some deep and dark clue to Quick's murder, I'm guessing."

"I wish I had seen it myself," she remarked. "I would have liked to cast my eye over these curious designs, if such they were."

"Well, the police still have it," I replied, "along with the rest of Quick's belongings. If we walked over to the police station, the inspector would willingly show it to you, I'm sure."

I saw that the proposition attracted her immediately. As with myself, Miss Raven felt the pull of fascination exercised upon people by the inspection of such strange criminal relics.

"Let's go, then," she said. "This afternoon. What do you say?"

I answered in the affirmative, equally keen to have another look at the tobacco box. Mr. Cazalette's hints about it, and his mysterious secrecy regarding his photographic experiments, had made me extra inquisitive. So after lunch that day Miss Raven and I walked across country to the police station, where we were shown into the presence of the inspector. Stood before him, I explained the nature of our visit.

On hearing it, the inspector gave a sceptical laugh. "You mean the thing that Mr. Cazalette was so keen on photographing? You don't mean to tell me his amateur studies have turned up something of note?"

"That is only known to Mr. Cazalette himself. He preserves a very strict silence on the subject," I answered. "It's that same secrecy that has piqued our further curiosity today."

"Well," remarked the inspector, indulgently, "it's a curiosity that can very easily be satisfied. I've got all Quick's belongings here—just as they were put together after being exhibited before the coroner."

Unlocking a cupboard in the corner of the room, he pointed to two bundles. The larger one was done up in linen; the other wrapped tightly with canvas. It was the second of the two that the inspector now reached for. "This contains his personal effects: money, watch, chain, and so forth. It's sealed, as you can see, but we'll put fresh seals on it after breaking these."

"It's very kind of you to take so much trouble," said Miss Raven. "All to satisfy a mere whim."

The inspector assured her that it was no trouble, and broke the seals of the small, carefully-wrapped package. There, neatly done up, were the dead man's effects, down to his pipe and pouch. His money was there: notes, gold, silver, and copper. There was a stump of lead pencil and a bit of string. Everything, in effect, except for one glaring omission. The tobacco box itself was nowhere in sight.

The inspector wore a look of utter perplexity. "I don't see it!" he exclaimed. "But how could that be?"

He turned the things over again, and yet again, without unearthing the tobacco box. Increasingly baffled—and aggrieved—he rang a bell and asked for a particular constable, who entered presently.

"Didn't you put these things together when the inquest was over?" demanded the inspector. "I told you to collect them up and bring them here and then seal them."

"I did, sir," answered the man, dismayed by his superior's implicit accusation. "I put together everything that was on the table at once. The package was never out of my hands till I got it here and sealed it. Sergeant Brown and myself counted the money as well."

"The money is all right," observed the inspector. "But there's a tobacco box missing. Do you remember seeing it at the time of inquest?"

"Can't say that I do, sir," replied the constable. "And I packed up everything that was there, as I've said."

The inspector signalled for him to leave again, then turned back to myself and Miss Raven, still pondering the mystery within a mystery. "That box must have been stolen at the time of the inquest," he reasoned. "But who could have done that? And, more to the point, why?"

10

It was evident that the inspector was considerably puzzled, not to say upset, by the disappearance of the tobacco box. I fancied that I saw the real reason for his sudden discomfiture. He had belittled Mr. Cazalette's avid interest in the item, and made light of mine and Miss Raven's own curiosity. Now, with its surreptitious theft—from under his very nose—he was angry with himself for his lack of care and perception.

In an effort to reassert his self-confidence, the inspector looked at me and nodded. "I can call to mind everybody who was sat round that tablet at the time of the inquest. You had two officials. There was our surgeon and Dr. Lorrimore. Also, three country gentlemen acting as magistrates—all of them well known to me. In addition, there were a couple of reporters at the foot of the table who I know well enough, too. Now who, out of that lot, would think to steal this tobacco box? And what would compel them to carry out such a senseless theft?"

"Well, there are those who have a morbid desire to possess mementoes of crime and criminals," I answered. "Indeed, I know one man who has a cabinet filled with sordid oddities—very proud of the fact that he owns a flute which once belonged to Charles Pease; a purse that was found on Frank Muller; a reputed riding-whip of Dick Turpin's. Perhaps one of these men is prone to some such mania, and appropriated the tobacco box as a memento of the Ravensdene Court slaying?"

"I don't know," replied the inspector. "But I think it unlikely. I know the lot of them, to a greater or lesser extent, and I think they've all too much sense."

"And you're sure that it was on the table at the time of the inquest?" I asked him.

"I am," he replied, "for I distinctly remember laying out the various objects myself prior to the start of proceedings."

"Then there's more to this matter than lies on the surface," said I.

"Evidently," he answered, looking from myself to Miss Raven, and back again. "I suppose the old gentleman, Mr. Cazalette, can be trusted? I mean, you don't think he's found out anything with his photography, and is keeping it back from plain view?"

"I know nothing of Mr. Cazalette except that he is a famous authority on coins and medals, a very remarkable person for his age, and a guest of Mr. Raven's," I answered. "As to his keeping the result of his investigations in the dark, I would not put it past him."

"Aye, so I guessed," muttered the inspector. "I wish he'd tell us, though, if he has discovered anything. But I suppose he'll act in his own sweet time as men of that age often do."

"By the way, if it's not a professional secret, have you heard any more of the affair at Saltash?" I asked him.

The inspector shook his head ruefully. "They've turned up nothing, either. That's as big a mystery as this!"

"What do you think of the two affairs, and their interconnection?" Miss Raven asked, ever more intrigued by the double mystery.

"I've given it a great deal of thought," he replied, "and it seems to me that the two brothers, Salter and Noah Quick, were men who had what's commonly called a past, and that there was some strange secret in it—probably one of money. I think that in their last days they were shadowed by some old associates of theirs, who murdered them in the expectation of serious profit. What I would really like to know is why did Salter Quick come down here to this particular bit of the North Country prior to his death?"

"To look for the graves of his ancestors on the mother's side. At least, that's what he told me," I answered.

"I know he did," remarked the inspector with an air of self-vindication. "And I've had the most careful inquires made with respect to the Netherfields. There isn't any such name in a churchyard, or parish register, between Alnmouth Bay and Fenham Flats—and that's a pretty good stretch of country! I set to work on those investigations as soon as you told me about your first meeting with Salter Quick."

"And yet it was not Salter Quick alone who was seeking the graves of the Netherfields," noted Miss Raven. "There was that other man, according to the drover, who had picked up the same scent."

The inspector turned to her and smiled appreciatively. "The most mysterious feature of the whole case in my own estimation! If only I could clap a hand on him——"

Sensing our interview was at an end, Miss Raven and I rose to leave and the inspector accompanied us to the door of the police station. As we were thanking him for his polite attentions, a man came along the street and paused close by us, looking inquiringly at the building from which we'd just emerged, and at our companion's smart semi-uniform. Finally, as we were about to turn away, he touched his cap.

"Begging your pardon," he said, "is this here the police office?"

Something in the man's tone made me look at him attentively. He was a shortish, thick-set man with a shock of sandy-red hair and three or four days' stubble on his cheeks and chin; and yet despite his unkempt appearance, a certain steadiness of gaze set him up as an honest fellow. His clothing was rough, and there were bits of straw, hay, and wood sticking out of it, as if he were well acquainted with the farming life.

"That it is," answered the inspector. "What can we do for you?"

The man looked up the steps with a glance in which there was a decided sense of humour.

"You'll not know me," he replied. "My name's Beeman— James Beeman—I come from near York as it happens. I should have called to see you before now, but I've been away up in the Cheviot Hills, out of reach."

"So what brings you here today?" asked the inspector amiably.

James Beeman showed a fine set of teeth in a grin that seemed to stretch completely across his homely face. "I'm the chap as was spoken of asking about the graves o' the Netherfield family. The fellow I chanced to meet outside Lesbury made mention of me, as I understand it."

The inspector turned to Miss Raven and myself with a look of plain astonishment. "Why, this is the very man we've just talked of!" Then, turning back to the newcomer, he assumed a more sober demeanour. "Please, come this way," he said, beckoning James Beeman inside the police station.

When all four of us were arranged about the inspector's room, he wasted no time in seeking further clarity. "I'm much obliged to you for coming. Now, what can you tell me about the grave of the Netherfields?"

Beeman laughed, shaking his head. Now that his tattered hat had been removed, the fiery hue of his hair was almost alarming in its crudeness.

"Nowt," he said. "Nowt at all! Or nothing much, at any rate."

"Go on," urged the inspector, as if willing him to contradict this last statement.

"Let me see now," Beeman continued. "I come up here on March sixth to see about some sheep stock for our maister, Mr. Dimbleby. The first night I put up at a temp'rance lodge in

Alnwick yonder. Of course, temp'rances is all right for sleeping and breakfasting, but not much good for owt else. So when I'd tea'd there, I went down the street to a comfortable public house, where I could smoke my pipe and have a glass or two. And while I was there, a man come in who, judging from his description in the papers, was that poor fellow what was murdered a week after . . . Now I didn't talk to him none, but after a bit I heard him conversing with the landlord. And after a deal o' talk about fishing hereabouts, I heard him asking the local man if he knew of any churchyards where the Netherfields might be buried. He talked so much about 'em that the name got fixed on my mind even after I'd left an hour later.

"The next day I had business outside Alnwick at one or two farms, and that night I made further north to put up at Embleton. Now as I were walking that way after dark, I chanced in wi' a man near Lesbury, and walked wi' him a piece, and asked him, finding he were a native, if he knew owt o' the Netherfield graves. That 'ud be the same man as told you that he'd met such a person. That's what I came here to clarify—that person happened to be me. . . "

"Then you merely asked the question out of curiosity?" said the inspector.

"Aye—just 'cause I'd heard that other fella inquire of it," assented Beeman. "I just wondered if it were some family o' consequence hereabouts."

"You never saw the man again whom you speak of as having seen at Alnwick?" the inspector asked him. "And had no direct conversation with him yourself?"

"Never saw the fellow again, nor had a single word with him," replied Beeman. "He had his glass or two o' rum, and went on his way. But I reckon he was the man who was murdered, all right."

"And where have you been yourself since the time of that incident?" asked the inspector.

"Right away across country," answered Beeman readily. "I went to Chillingham and Wooler, to some farms in the Cheviots, and then back by Alnham and Whittingham to Alnwick. It was then I heard all about this sorry business and thought to come and tell you what little I know."

"I'm much obliged to you, Mr. Beeman," said the inspector. "You've cleared up something, at any rate. Will you be long in the neighbourhood?"

"I shall be here for two or three days yet, collecting some sheep together," replied Beeman. "Then I shall be away. But if you ever want me, my directions is James Beeman, foreman to Mr. Thomas Dimbleby, Cross-houses Manor, York."

When this candid and direct person had gone, the inspector looked at Miss Raven and me with glances that indicated a good deal.

"That settles one point and seems to establish another," he remarked significantly. "Salter Quick was not murdered by somebody who'd come into these parts on the same errand as himself, but rather someone local to the area. It would seem that he crossed paths with a person here to whom his presence was so decidedly unwelcome that there was nothing for it but swift and certain murder. But who, of all the folk in these parts, is one to suspect?

Miss Raven and I took our leave for the second time, walking some distance from the police station before exchanging a word. I do not know what she was thinking of; as for myself, I was speculating on the change in my opinion brought about by the rough-and-ready statement of the brusque Yorkshireman. For until then I had firmly believed that the man who'd fallen in with Jim Gelthwaite, the drover, was the same man who'd murdered Salter Quick. Now that idea had been exploded, and, so far as I could see, the search for the real assassin was yet to begin.

Suddenly Miss Raven spoke. "I suppose it's scarcely possible that the murderer was present at that inquest?"

"Quite possible," said I. "The place was packed to the doors with all sorts of people, but why do you ask?"

"I thought perhaps he might have stolen away with the

tobacco box, knowing that as long as it was in the hands of the police there might be some clue to his identity," she suggested.

"It's a fair supposition," I replied. "There's just one thing against it, as far as I can fathom. If the murderer had known that, he'd have secured the box when he searched Quick's clothing, as he undoubtedly did."

"Of course!" she admitted. "I ought to have thought of that. But there are such a lot of things to consider in connection with this case—so many threads interwoven with each other."

I regarded her with concern and admiration in equal measure. "It's been weighing on your mind, quite clearly."

She made no reply for a moment, then tilted her head upwards to look at me. "It's not especially comforting to know that a brutal murder occurred at one's very door and that, for all one knows, the murderer may still be close at hand. Nor am I alone in this palpable disquiet —I know that Uncle Francis is frightfully upset by the situation."

"I hadn't observed that," I said.

"Perhaps not," she answered. "But he's an unusually nervous man, I can assure you. Do you know that since this happened he's taken to going round the house every night, examining doors and windows? In addition, he's started carrying a revolver as well."

I wondered why Mr. Raven should expect—or, if not expect, be afraid of—an attack on himself. But before I could make any comment on my companion's information, my attention was diverted. All that afternoon the weather had been threatening to break, and now, with startling suddenness, a flash of lightning was followed by a sharp crack of thunder. Within a couple of seconds, a heavy downpour of rain also commenced.

I glanced at Miss Raven's light dress. Early spring though it was, the weather had been warm for more than a week, and she had come out in things that would be soaked through in a moment. As I saw, we were close to an old red-brick house, a few yards back from the road, and divided from it by nothing more

than a strip of garden. It had a deep doorway, and without ceremony, I pushed open the little gate in front and drew Miss
Raven within its shelter. We had not stood there long, with our
back to the door, when a soft mellifluous voice sounded close to
my startled ear.

"Will you not step inside and shelter from the storm?"

Twisting round sharply, I found myself staring at the enigmatic countenance of a man from the far East.

❧ 11 ❧

Had Miss Raven and I been caught up out of that little coastal village and transported on a magic carpet—to be set down in the twinkling of an eye upon some Oriental threshold—we could scarcely have been more surprised by the man's sudden appearance. For the moment I was at a loss to think who and what he might be. He was in the dress of his own country, wearing a neat, close-fitting, high-buttoned blue jacket, a small cap, with a black pigtail trailing away behind it. I was not sufficiently acquainted with Chinese costumes to gather any idea of his rank or position. For aught I knew, he might be a mandarin who, for some extraordinary reason, had found his way to this out-of-the-world spot. For all of these reasons, my answer to his courteous invitation no doubt sounded confused and awkward.

"Oh, thank you," I said, "pray don't let us put you to any trouble. If we may just stand under your porch a moment—"

He stood a little aside, waving us politely into the hall behind him.

"Dr. Lorrimore would be very angry with me if I allowed a lady and gentleman to stand in his door and did not invite them into his house," he said, in the same even, mellifluous tones.

"Oh, is this Dr. Lorrimore's residence?" I said. "Thank you—then we will come in. Is the doctor at home presently?"

The man shook his head courteously. "He's in the village, but I expect him back any moment."

After closing the door, and passing us with a polite bow, our guide preceded us along the hall before throwing open the door of a room which looked out on a trim garden. Still smiling, he invited us to be seated, and then, with another bow, left the room silently.

Miss Raven and I glanced at each other.

"So Dr. Lorrimore has a Chinese man servant?" she said. "How extraordinary! Well, no doubt he feels at home here," she continued, looking about her. "After all, this is a bit Oriental."

Miss Raven was right in that. The room into which we'd been ushered was certainly suggestive of what one heard of India. There were fine rugs on the floor, ivories and brasses in the cabinets, and the curtains were of fabric that could only have come out of some Eastern bazaar. In the air, there was a curious scent of sandalwood and dried rose petals. And on the mantel-piece, where one might have expected to find a marble clock, reposed a menacing Hindu god, wrathful in appearance, whose baleful eyes seemed to follow all our movements.

"Yes," I admitted, reflectively. "Having been in India for some years, Dr. Lorrimore appears to have brought plenty of its ways and means back with him."

"I suppose this is his drawing-room," said Miss Raven. "Now, if only it looked out on palm-trees, and all those other things one associates with India."

"Just so," said I. "What it does look out on, however, is a typical English garden on which, at present, about a ton of rain is descending."

"Oh, but it won't keep on like that for long," she said. "And I suppose, if it does, then Dr. Lorrimore might have a car that he can lend us."

"I don't think that's very likely," said I. "The country practitioner is usually more dependent on a bicycle than a brougham. But here he is, so we can at least ask."

I had just caught sight of Lorrimore as he entered his garden by a door set in its ivy-covered wall. He ran hastily up the path to the house, and, within a minute or two, had opened the door of our room after divesting himself of his mackintosh.

"So glad you were near enough to turn in here for shelter!" he exclaimed, shaking hands with us warmly. "I see that neither of you expected rain—I went out prepared, as you can see."

"We made for the first door we saw," said Miss Raven. "But we had no idea it was yours, Dr. Lorrimore. And do tell me," she continued in a whisper, "is that your man-servant we met before?"

Lorrimore laughed, rubbing his hands together. That day he was not in the solemn finery in which he'd visited Ravensdene Court; instead he wore a suit of grey tweed which made him look rather younger and less impressive. But he was certainly no ordinary man, and as he stood there smiling at Miss Raven's eager face, I felt conscious that he was the sort of mysterious, elusive figure in which women would naturally be interested.

"Man-servant hardly does justice to Wing's wide array of roles and capabilities. He's a model cook, valet, launderer, general factotum—there's nothing that he can't do or won't do. From making the most perfect curries to dealing with tradesmen, he's an absolute treasure. You could go the round of this house at any moment, without finding a thing out of place, or a single speck of dust in any one corner."

"You brought him from India, I suppose?" said I.

"Yes, I did," the doctor replied. "He'd already been with me for some time before I left, so we're thoroughly used to each other."

"And does he really like living here?" asked Miss Raven. "In such absolutely different surroundings?"

Lorrimore gave another laugh. "Wing is an old hand at making the best of the moment. A philosopher, in short. One who has his own pronounced notions of happiness. At present he's supremely happy in getting you some tea, which I'm sure you're going to enjoy. You mightn't think it, but this man from the East can make an English plum-cake that would put the swellest London pastry-cook to shame!"

The Chinaman presently summoned us to tea, which he'd laid out in Lorrimore's dining-room. In contrast to the first room, it was eminently Victorian: an affair of heavy furniture and steel engravings, with old family plate arrayed on the long wooden sideboard. After ushering us in with all due ceremony, Wing closed the door tactfully behind him.

Lorrimore gave us an arch glance.

"You see how readily and skilfully that chap adapts himself to the needs of the moment," he said admiringly. "Now, you mightn't think it, but this is the very first time I have ever been honoured with visitors to afternoon tea. Observe how Wing immediately falls in with English taste and custom! Without a word from me, out comes the silver tea-pot, the best china, the finest linen! He produces his choicest plum-cake; the bread-and-butter is cut with wafer-like thinness; and the tea—ah, well, no Englishwoman, Miss Raven, can make a pot of tea to match!"

"It's quite plain that you've got a treasure in your house, Dr. Lorrimore," said Miss Raven. "But then, the Chinese are a very clever people, aren't they?"

"Remarkable, indeed," assented our host. "Shrewd, observant, penetrative. I have often wondered if this man of mine would find any great difficulty in seeing through a brick wall if it pleased him to!"

"He would be a useful person, perhaps, in solving the present mystery," said I. "The police seem to have got no further."

"Ah, the Quick business," remarked Lorrimore off-handedly. "Well, as regards that, it seems to me that whatever light is thrown on it will have to come from Devonport. From all that I've gathered, it's evident that what is really wanted is a strict examination into the immediate happenings at Noah Quick's inn. But is there anything fresh? You sound well informed. Have any new development to share with me?"

I told him briefly all that had happened that afternoon—of the information given by James Beeman, and of the disappearance of the tobacco box.

"That's odd!" he remarked. "Let's see—it was the old gentleman I saw at Ravensdene Court who had some fancy about that box, wasn't it?"

I nodded in reply "Mr. Cazalette saw, or fancied he saw, certain marks or scratches within the lid of the box which he took to have some meaning. They were, he firmly believed, made to some purpose. He thought that by photographing them, and then enlarging his photograph, he would bring out those marks more clearly and possibly find out what they were really meant for."

"Yes?" said Lorrimore with distinct interest. "Well—what has he discovered?"

"Up to now nobody knows," said Miss Raven. "Mr. Cazalette won't tell us anything."

"Sounds as if he's chanced on something," observed Lorrimore. "Perhaps he's suddenly going to let loose a tremendous theory and wants to perfect it before he speaks. Oh, well," added the doctor, almost indifferently, "I've known a good many murder mysteries in my time—out in India—and I always found that the best way of getting to the bottom of them was to go as far back as possible. If I were the police in charge of these cases, I should put one question down before me and do nothing until I'd exhausted every effort to solve it."

"And that would be what?" I asked.

"What were the personal histories of Noah and Salter Quick?"

"You think they had a past?" Miss Raven asked.

"Everybody has a past," answered Lorrimore. "It may be this, it may be that, but nearly all the problems of the present have their origin and solution in yesteryear. Find out what and where those two middle-aged men had been in their time, and then there'll be a chance to work forward."

The rain cleared off after we'd finished tea, and presently Miss Raven and I took our leave of the doctor. Lorrimore informed us that Mr. Raven had asked him to dinner on the following evening; he would accordingly see us again very soon.

"It will be quite an event for me!" he said gaily, as he opened the garden gate. "I live like an anchorite in this place. The local folk are scandalously healthy and I rarely get to practise any medicine! It's just as well my scientific investigations occupy me more often then not."

"At least, you have a treasure of a servant," observed Miss Raven. "Please tell him that his plum-cake was absolute perfection."

The Chinaman was just then standing at the open door, waiting on his master. Miss Raven threw him a laughing nod, to which he responded with a deep bow, before we turned and departed with that curious picture in our minds: of Lorrimore, essentially English in spite of his long residence in the East; and of his suave, smiling helpmate.

"A curious pair and a strange combination!" I remarked as we walked away. "That house, at any rate, has a plenitude of brain-power within it. What amazes me is that a clever chap like Master Wing should be content to bury his talents in such an unassuming foreign place, merely to make curries and plum-cake!"

"Perhaps he has a faithful devotion to his master," said Miss Raven. "Anyway, it's romantic and picturesque to find a real live Chinaman in an English village. I wonder if the poor man gets teased about his exotic clothes and pigtail?"

"Didn't Lorrimore say he was a philosopher?" said I. "There-fore he'll be indifferent to criticism. And I dare say he doesn't go about much."

That the Chinaman was not quite a recluse, however, I discovered a day or two later. This was after I went along the headlands, taking a solitary stroll after a stiff day's work in the library. Turning into the Mariner's Joy for a glass of Claigue's undeniably good ale, Wing was just coming out of the house as I entered it. He was as neat and friendly as before, although armed now with a very large umbrella, and carrying a sizeable basket filled with small parcels that suggested a shopping expedition. Greeting me with a respectful smile, he soon went on his way.

On entering the inn, I found its landlord alone in his bar-parlour.

"You no doubt have a colourful clientele, Mr. Claigue," I observed as he attended to my modest wants. "Yet it's not often, I should think, that a real live Chinaman walks in on you."

"He's been in two or three times, that one," replied Claigue. "Chinaman he is, no doubt, sir, but it strikes me he must know as much of this country as he knows of his own, for he speaks our tongue like a native."

"He has been in Dr. Lorrimore's service for some years," I answered. "No doubt he's had abundant opportunities of picking up the language. Still, it's an odd sight to see a Chinaman, pigtail and all, in these parts, isn't it?"

"Well, I've had all sorts in here, time and again," replied Claigue reflectively. "Sailor men, mostly. But of all the lot, that poor chap as got knifed the other week was the most mysterious by far. What do you make of it, Mr. Middlebrook?"

"I don't know what to make of it," said I. "I don't think anybody knows what to make of it. The police don't, anyhow!"

"The police!" he exclaimed, with a note of derision. "They're worse than a parcel of old women! Just a bit of surface inquiry, and nothing more than that. My notion is that the police don't care the value of that match whether the thing's ever cleared up or not. Still—there's a good deal of talk about."

"I expect you hear plenty of it in this parlour of yours?" I reasoned.

"Nights—yes," he said in agreement. "A murder's always a good subject of conversation. At first, those who come in here of an evening could talk of naught else, floating this and that theory. It's died down a fair bit, to be sure, but there's still a good deal of idle speculation."

"And what's the general opinion?" I inquired. "I suppose there is one?"

"I wouldn't say that," he answered thoughtfully. "Opinions hereabouts are wildly varied; not to say, fantastical."

"In what way?" I asked.

"Well," said he with a laugh, "there is one that comes nearer to being what you might call general than any of the others. There's a party of the older men that come here who're dead certain that Quick was murdered by a woman!"

"A woman!" I exclaimed. "Whatever makes them think that?"

"Those footmarks," answered Claigue. "You'll remember, Mr. Middlebrook, that there were two sets of prints in the sand thereabouts. One was certainly Quick's—they fitted his boots. The other was very delicate, made by some light-footed person. Well, some of the folk hereabouts went along to Kernwick Cove the day of the murder, and looked at those prints. They say the lighter ones were made by a woman."

I let my recollections go back to the morning on which I'd found Quick lying dead on the patch of yellow sand.

"Of course," I said reflectively, "those marks are long gone now."

"Aye!" exclaimed Claigue. "There's been a good many tides washed over that spot since the time of that foul murder. But they haven't washed out the fact that a man's life was let out there! And whether it was man or woman that stuck that knife into the poor fellow's shoulders, it'll come out some day."

"I'm not so sure ," said I. "There's a goodly percentage of unsolved murders that are still outstanding."

"Murder will out," Claigue declared. "I still have faith in that old saying. What I don't like is the notion that the murderer may still be walking about this quarter, free and unsuspected.

Why, I may even have served him with a glass of beer! What's to prevent it? Murderers don't carry a label on their foreheads!"

"What do you think the police ought to do?" I asked him.

"I think they should start working backward," he replied decisively. "I read all I could in the newspapers, and I came to the conclusion that there was a secret behind those two brothers. Both murdered on the same night, hundreds of miles apart—that's no common crime, Mr Middlebrook! Who were these men? What was their past history? That's what the police ought to have busied themselves with to date."

It was the second time I had heard that advice in quick succession, and I returned to Ravensdene Court, still reflecting on it. Who, after all, were Noah and Salter Quick, and what was their life-story? I was still wondering how these things could be brought to light when I passed the door to Mr. Cazalette's room on my way down to dinner. Without warning, the door opened and he stood on the threshold, looking left and right, before cautiously ushering me in.

"Middlebrook," he whispered—though he had by then shut the door—"you're a sensible lad, and so I'll acquaint you with a matter. This very morning, as I was taking my regular dip, my pocket-book was stolen out of the jacket that I'd left on shore."

"Was there anything of great value in it?" I asked.

Cazalette paused, then nodded meaningfully.

"It contained a clue pertaining to yon man's murder—make of that what you will!"

❧ 12 ❧

I sensed that Mr. Cazalette was about to open up and explain his own somewhat mysterious doings on the morning of the murder. Awaiting this revelation, an excited curiosity rose in me. I think the old man saw it, for he signalled for me to sit down in an easy chair while he perched on the very edge of his single bed.

"Sit you down, Middlebrook," he said. "We've some time yet before dinner, and I'm wanting to talk to you in private. There's things I'm not willing—as yet—to tell everybody, but I'll share them with you and we'll take a bit of counsel together. As I said, my pocket-book contained a clue to the identity of the man that murdered yon Salter Quick, as best I understand it. Of course, I should have taken more care, but who'd have thought it would be stolen from under my very nose while I was out taking my morning dip? If nothing else, it serves as more evidence that there's some uncommonly sharp and clever criminals abroad in the area."

"And you're positive that you had it with you while you were bathing, Mr. Cazalette?"

He turned on his bed, pointing to a venerable Norfork jacket which hung on a peg in a recess by the washstand. I knew it well enough: I had often seen him in it first thing of a morning.

"It's my custom," said he, "to array myself in that old coatie when I go for my dip. It's thick and warm, and I've had it twenty years or more—good tweed it is, and homespun. And whenever I've gone out there of a morning, I've put my pocket-book in the inside pocket, and laid the coat itself and the rest o' my scanty attire on the bank there down at Kernwick Cove. Well, I did the very same thing this morning—and when I came to my clothes again, the pocket-book was gone!"

"You saw nobody about?" I asked.

"Nobody," said he. "But Lord, man, I know how easy it was to do the thing! You'll bear in mind that on the right hand side of that cove, the grasses comes right down to the edge of the cliff. A man lurking amongst the undergrowth would have nothing to do but reach his arm to the bank, draw my coatie to his nefarious self, and abstract my property. And by the time I was on dry land again, and wanting my garments, he'd be a quarter of a mile away!"

"And the clue?" I asked.

He edged a little nearer to me, and dropped his voice still lower.

"If you'll let your mind go back to the morning when you found Quick lying dead on the sand, you might remember that before ever you were down at the place, I'd been there before you. You might wonder then why I didn't find what you found. Well, I took a different route, as is my habit. There's many big rocks and boulders standing well up on that beach, and one or other of them must have obscured my point of view. Anyway, I didn't find Salter Quick, but I did find something that maybe had to do with his murder."

"What, Mr. Cazalette?" I asked, though by now I knew well enough what he was talking of. Now I wanted him to say, and have done with it: his circumlocution was getting wearisome.

But he was one of those old men who won't allow their cattle to be hurried, and went on in his long-winded way.

"You'll be aware," he continued, "that there's a deal of gorse and bramble growing right down to the very edge of the coast thereabouts. If it catches anything loose, anything protruding from the pocket of a garment, it'll lay hold and stick to it. Well on one of those bushes, I saw fluttering in the morning breeze a soiled handkerchief with two sorts of stains upon it. One caused by the soft mud of the adjacent beach, the other being a smear of blood as if somebody had wiped the blood from their fingers. But it was not the blood, per se, that prompted me to pick it up betwixt thumb and forefinger. Rather, I saw at once that this was no common man's property, for there was a crest woven into one corner, and a monogram of initials underneath it. It wasn't linen—though it looked like it at first—and nor was it silk either, for I'm well acquainted with that fabric. Maybe it was a mixture of the two, but it had not been woven or made in any British factory: the thing was distinctly of foreign origin."

"What were the markings you speak of?" I asked.

"The crest consisted of a coronet, or that make of thing, and had been woven in one corner. And the letters beneath it were a V and a de and a C. Man! That handkerchief was the property of some man of quality, and no mistaking! And the stains being wet —the mud-stains, at any rate, though the smear of blood was dry —I gathered that it had been but recently deposited. The man who'd left it there had used it on the beach, I supposed—maybe he'd cut his toe bathing, or something o' that sort, or cut his finger gathering a shell or fossil. After that, he must have thrust it carelessly into a side-pocket for a thorn to catch hold of as he passed. But there it was, all the same, and chance dictated that I find it."

"And what did you do with it, Mr. Cazalette?" I inquired with seeming innocence.

"I slipped it among my towels to bring back to the house, but on the way I thought it might cause the maids to wonder. Therefore, I thrust it into a hedge as I was passing along, thinking to go back and examine it at my leisure. And when I'd got myself dressed, I did go back and take it, placing it within a stout envelope. It was then that you came along, Middlebrook, with your story of the murder, and I saw then that before saying a word to anybody, I'd keep my own counsel and examine that thing more carefully. And man alive! I've no doubt whatever that the man who left the handkerchief behind him was the man who knifed Salter Quick!"

"I gather from all you've said, that the handkerchief was in the pocket-book you had stolen this morning?"

"You're right in that," said he. "It was. Wrapped up in a bit of oiled paper, and in a sealed down envelope with the date and particulars of my discovery written upon it. Also letters and papers of my own, and a trifling amount of money. But there was yet another thing that, in view of all we know, may be a serious thing to have fall into the hands of evildoers. A print, Middlebrook, of the enlarged photograph I made of the inside of yon dead man's tobacco box!"

He regarded me with intense seriousness as he made this announcement. Not knowing exactly what to say, I remained silent.

"Aye!" he continued. "And it's my distinct and solemn belief that it was this the thief was after! Ye see, Middlebrook, it's been spoken of widely that I was interested in those marks on the inside of that lid, and got the police to let me make a photograph. That's why I think there's somebody about who's keenly anxious to know what I learned as a result."

"You really think so?" I asked.

"Aye, man, this was no common murder any more than the murder of the man's own brother down yonder at Saltash. We're living in the very midst of a mystery—and its sinister authors remain close by."

"I thought you believed that Salter Quick's murderer was miles away before his body was cold?"

"I did, " he answered: "but I've changed my mind since I was robbed of my venerable pocket-book."

"And was the print in your pocket-book the only one you possess?"

"It wasn't," he said with evident satisfaction. "If the thief thought he was securing something unique, he was wholly mistaken. However, I still didn't want him, or anybody else, to get hold of even one print, for as sure as we're living men, Middlebrook, what was on the inside of that lid was a key to something!"

"You forget that the tobacco box itself was stolen from the police's safekeeping," I reminded him.

"I don't forget anything of the sort," he retorted. "And the fact you've mentioned it makes me all the more assured, my man, that what I say is correct! There's him, or there's them—in all likelihood it's the plural—that's uncommonly anxious to unravel this secret. What were Salter Quick's pockets turned out for? What were the man's clothes slashed and hacked at? Why did the killer of Noah Quick at Saltash treat the man in similar fashion? It wasn't money the two men were murdered for—no, it was information."

"And you truly believe that this key is in the marks or scratches or whatever they are on the lid of the tobacco box?" I asked.

"Aye, I do!" he exclaimed. "And what's more, Middlebrook, I believe I'm a darned fool for the way I've gone about proving it! If I'd contrived to get a good, careful look at that box without saying anything to the police, it might very well have escaped the thief's attention. Instead I spoke my thoughts aloud before a company, and made a present of them to these miscreants. Until I said what I did, the murderous gang that knifed yon two men hadn't a notion that Salter Quick carried a key in the shape of his tobacco box."

"You don't mean to suggest that the murderers were present when you asked permission to photograph the box!" I exclaimed.

Cazalette give a non-committal shrug. "I'm not saying that any of the gang were present in Raven's outhouse yonder, but there were a dozen or more men heard what I said to the police inspector, and saw me taking my photograph. And men talk—no matter of what degree they are."

"Mr. Cazalette," said I, "I would like to see your results, if I may."

He got off his bed at that, and going over to a chest of drawers, unlocked one, and took out a writing case from which he presently extracted a sheet of cardboard. Thereon he had mounted a photograph, beneath which were some lines of explanatory writing. This he placed in my hand without a word, watching me silently as I looked at it.

I could make nothing of the thing. It looked to me like a series—a very small one—of meaningless scratches, evidently made with the point of a knife, or a strong pin, on the surface of the metal. Certainly, the marks were there, and looked to have been made with some intent, but it's true nature still escaped me.

"What d'ye make of it, lad?" he inquired after a while. "Anything?"

"Nothing, Mr. Cazalette," I replied adamantly. "Nothing whatsoever."

"It's a plan, Middlebrook," he answered. "A plan of some place. But I can't say any more than that. I've speculated a great deal on the meaning and significance of those lines and marks, but without further success."

"To some place that Salter Quick knew of?" I suggested.

"Aye, and that somebody else wants to know of as well."

"It's true they've got—or somebody's got—your pocketbook," I answered. "But this, and the handkerchief, might not have been the thief's main object. It must be pretty well known that you go down to the beach to bathe every morning, and are in the habit of leaving your clothes about. Maybe a common garden thief sought to take advantage."

My theory exercised the old man and he shook his head forcefully.

"No—I'm not with you, Middlebrook!" he said. "Somewhere around us there's what I say—crafty and bloody murderers! Mark my words, we haven't heard the last of them yet!"

Just then the dinner bell rang, and he put the photographic print away, and we went downstairs together. That was the evening on which Dr. Lorrimore was to dine with us, and we found him in the hall, talking to Mr. Raven and his niece. Joining them, we found that their subject of conversation was the same that had just engaged Mr. Cazalette and myself. It turned out that the police inspector had been round to Lorrimore's house, inquiring if Lorrimore had noticed that now missing and all-important object at the time of the inquest.

"Of course I saw it!" remarked Lorrimore, narrating this fact to us. "I told him I not only saw it, but handled it as well, as did several other people. Mr. Cazalette here had drawn attention to the thing when we were examining the dead man, and there was therefore open interest in the item." (Here Mr. Cazalette, standing close by me, nudged my elbow, to remind me of what he'd said minutes earlier.) "And I told the inspector something else, or, rather, put him in mind of something he'd evidently forgotten," continued Lorrimore. "That inquest was attended by a good many strangers, who had evidently been attracted by mere curiosity. There were a lot of people there who certainly did not belong to this neighbourhood. And when the proceedings were over, they came crowding round that table, morbidly inquisitive about the dead man's belongings. What could have been easier, as I said to the inspector, than for some one of them —perhaps a curio-hunter—to quietly pick up that box and make off with it? There are people who'd give a good deal to lay hold of a souvenir of that sort."

Mr. Raven muttered something about there being no accounting for tastes, and then we went in to dinner and began to talk of less gruesome things. Lorrimore was a brilliant and accomplished conversationalist, and the time passed pleasantly until, as we men were lingering a little over our wine, and Miss Raven was softly playing the piano in the adjoining drawing-room, the butler came in and whispered to his master.

Raven turned an astonished face to the rest of us.

"The police inspector is here now," he said, "and with him a detective from Devonport. They are anxious to see me—and you, Middlebrook. The detective has something to tell."

❧ 13 ☙

I am not sure which of us sitting at that table had ever come into personal contact with a detective—I myself had never met one in my life—but Mr. Raven's announcement excited much curiosity. Miss Raven caught her uncle's last words from the adjoining room, the door of which was open, and hastened in expectantly. I think she, like most of us, wondered what sort of being we were about to see.

Possibly there was a shade of disappointment on her face when the police inspector walked in followed by a small, rotund, rather merry-faced man who looked more like a prosperous cheesemonger or successful draper than an emissary of justice. He was just the sort of person you would expect to see with an apron round his comfortable waistline or a pencil stuck in his ear.

"Sorry to disturb you, Mr. Raven," said the inspector with an apologetic bow as his companion followed behind him. "But we are anxious to have a little talk with you and Mr. Middlebrook. This is Mr. Scarterfield, from the police at Devonport, who has been placed in charge of the Noah Quick investigation."

Mr. Raven murmured some commonplace about being glad to see his visitors, and, with his usual hospitality, offered them both refreshment. We made room for them at the table at which we were sitting, and some of us, I think, were impatient to hear what Mr. Scarterfield had to tell. But the detective was evidently one of those men who readily adapt themselves to whatever company they are thrown into. He betrayed no eagerness to get to business until he had lighted one of Mr. Raven's cigars and toasted his host with a whisky and soda. It was only then, fully at his ease, he turned a friendly, all-embracing smile on the rest of us.

"I had better start by telling you how far my investigations have gone," he said amiably. "Then we shall know precisely where we are, and from what point we can, perhaps, make a new departure now that I have come here. I was put in charge of this case—at least of the Saltash murder—from the very beginning, but needless to say events here directly pertain to it. "

Mr. Cazalette, on hearing this, gave a loud grunt of assent.

"So when the news came through about Salter Quick, it seemed to me that the first thing to do was to find out a very pertinent thing—who were the brothers Quick?" the detective continued. "What was in their past, immediate or otherwise, that might prompt this unlikely double murder? A pretty stiff proposition, as you may readily guess, for each was a man of mystery. No one in our quarter knew anything more of Noah Quick than that he had come to Devonport some little time previous, taken over the license of the Admiral Parker, conducted his house very well, and had the reputation of being a quiet, reserved sort of man who was making good money. As to Salter, nobody knew anything except that he had been visiting Noah for some time. The two men evidently had no other family ties, for not a soul has come forward to claim relationship, despite the wide publicity."

"Do you think Quick was their real name?" asked Mr. Cazalette, who from the first had been listening with rapt attention. "Perhaps it was an assumed one?"

"I had thought of that," replied Scarterfield, "but you must remember that full descriptions of the two brothers appeared in the press, and that portraits of both were printed alongside it. Nobody came forward, and yet there was a powerful inducement for any relations to appear, never mind whether they were Quick, or Brown, or Smith, or Robinson."

"Aye!" said Mr. Cazalette. "And that was——"

"Money!" said the detective, beating him to the punchline. "If these men left any relations, I dare say they would have come forward and claimed their estates. No, I firmly believe now that these two hadn't another blood relation in the world, strange as that might be."

"So the brothers were as prosperous as they appeared?" I asked.

Scarterfield nodded. "Inquiries were made of Noah Quick's solicitors and bankers. The solicitors knew nothing about him except that he'd employed them now and then in trifling matters, and that of late he'd composed a will which made Salter his sole heir. About the same time they'd also made a will for Salter, in which he bequeathed everything he had to Noah.

"Then I approached the bankers and learned that Noah Quick had deposited a considerable sum of money on arrival in Devonport. At the time of his death, he had several thousand pounds lying there to his credit. His bankers also had charge of several valuable securities. On Salter Quick's coming to the Admiral Parker, Noah introduced him to this bank, where Salter deposited a sum of about two thousand pounds in addition. He also left some valuable scrip and securities, chiefly of Indian railways. Altogether, those bankers hold a lot of money that belongs to the two brothers."

"The mystery deepens," said Mr Cazalette, not without relish.

The detective nodded his head in full agreement. "There are certain indications that they made their money in the far East, but neither brother was forthcoming on this matter. The only man I have come across who can give me the faintest idea of anything respecting their past is a regular frequenter of the Admiral Parker. He says that he once gathered from Salter Quick that he and Noah were natives of Rotherhithe, and that they were orphans and the last of their lot."

"And have you have been there, to Rotherhithe, pursuing your inquiries?" asked Mr. Raven.

"I have, sir," replied Scarterfield, "although I found nothing of any help to me. If the two brothers lived there at one time, they must have been taken as children and born elsewhere. Nor could I come across anybody at all who knew anything of them in seafaring circles thereabouts. I came to the conclusion that whoever these two men were, and whatever they had been, most of their lives had been spent away from this country."

"Probably in the far East, as you previously suggested," muttered Mr. Cazalette.

"Likely," agreed Scarterfield. "Their money would seem to have been made there, judging by their securities at any rate."

"But other than that," I added, "there's nothing more that can be safely said?"

My question earned me an enigmatic smile that hinted at further knowledge. "Well, there's more ways than one of finding things out, and after I'd knocked round a good deal of Thames' side, I turned my attention to Lloyds the insurers. Now connected with Lloyds are various publications having to do with shipping matters—the 'Weekly Shipping Index' and the 'Confidential Index' among them. With time and patience, you can find out a great deal not only about ships, but also the men who once sailed in them. And to cut a long story short, I did at last get a clue about Noah and Salter Quick last week."

Here the detective paused, producing from his breast-pocket a small bundle of papers which he laid before him on the table. I suppose we all gazed at them as if they suggested deep and dark mystery, but for the time being Scarterfield let them lie idle where he had placed them.

"In October, 1907, now nearly five years ago, a certain steam ship, the *Elizabeth Robinson*, left Hong-Kong for Chemulpo, one of the principal ports in Korea. She was spoken of in the Yellow Sea, several days later, but after that she was never heard of again. According to the information available at Lloyds, she probably went down in a typhoon and was totally lost, as were all crew and cargo. From all that I could gather, she was merely a tramp steamer that did odd jobs anywhere between India and China, and had seen a good deal of active service. All the same, she's of considerable interest to me, for I have managed to secure a list of the names of the men who were on her when she left Hong-Kong for Chemulpo. And amongst those names, Noah and Salter Quick both appear . . ."

"Yet Noah and Salter Quick were still alive less than a month ago," asserted Mr. Raven.

Scarterfield slipped off the india-rubber band which confined his papers, and selecting one, slowly unfolded it. "Just so, sir!" he agreed, dryly. "So either the *Elizabeth Robinson* did not go down in a typhoon, or else the two brothers somehow escaped the full brunt of its fury. Whichever is the case, here is a list of the men who were aboard when she set sail from Hong-Kong. And here are the names of Noah Quick and Salter Quick, both set down as passengers. It also includes a captain and a crew of eighteen, which didn't seem to have any special relevance, except in two instances. The first of these exceptions, Mr. Middlebrook, should be of particular interest to you."

"How so?" I asked, my intense curiosity further excited.

"It's Netherfield," said the detective, calmly.

"Netherfield!" I exclaimed

Scarterfield nodded triumphally. "William Netherfield, a deck-hand who hailed from Blyth, right here in Northumberland as I understand it. That's the name on the list of those who were aboard the *Elizabeth Robinson* when she left Hong-Kong and disappeared from sight."

"From Blyth?" remarked Mr. Cazalette. "The same Blyth that lies some miles southward of here?"

"That's right," said Scarterfield, "which is why I propose to visit the place in short order. But I hope you appreciate the extraordinary coincidence, gentlemen. In October, 1907, Salter Quick is on a tramp steamer in the Yellow Sea, more or less intimate with a sailor-man from Blyth whose name is Netherfield. In March, 1912, he is on the sea-coast near Alnmouth, asking if anybody knows of a churchyard in these parts where people of the name of Netherfield are buried? So what had the man Netherfield who was with Salter Quick in Chinese waters in 1907 got to do with Salter Quick's presence here five years later?"

Nobody attempted to answer these questions, but presently I added one more.

"You spoke of two names on the list as striking you with some significance," I said. "Netherfield is one. What is the other?"

"That of a Chinaman," replied Scarterfield, referring to his documents. "Set down as cook. Chuh Fen is the name given. And why it's significant to me is because of something else I learnt during the course of my inquiries. Three years ago, a Chinaman of the same name dropped in at Lloyds and was anxious to know if the steamer *Elizabeth Robinson*, which sailed from Hong-Kong for Chemulpo, ever arrived at its destination. He was given the same information that was afforded me, and on receiving it, went away silently. Now then—was this the same Chuh Fen who was also on the *Elizabeth Robinson*? If so, how did he escape the resulting shipwreck or whatever fate befell the vessel? And why did he want to know, after two years' lapse of time, if the ship really did reach Chemulpo safely?" Scarterfield shook his head, still perplexed by the trio of questions. "I only wish I'd chanced to be at Lloyds when Chuh Fen called there."

Something impelled Miss Raven and myself to glance at Dr. Lorrimore at that point. He nodded, knowing what we were thinking of, and duly addressed Scarterfield.

"I happen to have a Chinaman in my employ at present—a very clever man who has been in my employ for several years."

The detective turned an interested glance on the physician. "And do you live hereabouts, sir? I don't think I caught your name before."

"This is Dr. Lorrimore—our neighbour," said Mr. Raven hurriedly.

I think Lorrimore saw what had suddenly come into Scarterfield's mind, which prompted from him a sceptical laugh, defensive in nature.

"Don't get the idea that my man Wing had anything to do with the murder of Salter Quick!" he said passionately. "I can vouch for him and his movements—I know exactly where he was on the night of the murder. That said, he's a man of infinite resource and superior intelligence, and might therefore be of use to you in tracing this Chuh Fen character. After our return from India, previous to my coming here, Wing paid a good many visits to his fellow Chinamen in the East End. He also had a holiday in Liverpool, and another at Cardiff, where I am told there are Chinese settlements as well. And I happen to know that he carries on extensive correspondence with his compatriots. If you think he could give you any information, Mr. Scarterfield, I will gladly place him at your disposal."

"I'd like to have a talk with him, certainly," responded the detective, with some eagerness.

Lorrimore turned to Mr. Raven.

"If your coachman could run across with the dog-cart, and tell Wing that I want him, he'll be here in a jiffy. He may also be able to suggest something with regard to the *Elizabeth Robinson*. Before I picked him up in Bombay, he had knocked about the ports of the Yellow Sea."

🙊 14 🙈

After half an hour had passed, behind the somewhat pompous figure of the butler, I watched Wing enter. Invited to take a seat at one end of the table, the Chinaman deported himself gracefully. I do not know what the rest thought, but it lay in my own mind that if there was one man in that room who might be trusted to find his way out of the maze in which we were wandering, that man was Dr. Lorrimore's servant.

It was Lorrimore who, at the detective's request, explained to Wing why we had sent for him. The Chinaman nodded a grave assent when reminded of the Salter Quick affair—evidently he knew all about it. And—if one really could detect anything at all in so carefully veiled a countenance—I thought I could discern an increased watchfulness in his eyes when Scarterfield began to ask him questions.

"There is evidence," began the detective, "that this man Salter Quick, and his brother Noah, were mixed up in some affair that had connection with a trading steamer, the *Elizabeth Robinson*. One that is believed to have been lost in the Yellow Sea, between Hong-Kong and Chemulpo, in October 1907. On board that steamer was a certain Chinaman, who, two years later, turned up in London. Now, Dr. Lorrimore tells me that you spent a good deal of time amongst your own people in the East End, and that you also visited some of them in Liverpool and Cardiff. So I want to ask you—did you ever hear, in any of these quarters, of a man known as Chuh Fen?"

The Chinaman moved his head very slightly.

"No," he answered. "Not in London—nor in England. But I knew a man named Chuh Fen eleven years ago, before I went to Bombay and entered my present service."

"Where did you know him?" asked Scarterfield.

"Two—perhaps three places," said Wing. "Singapore, Penang, perhaps Rangoon, too."

"What was he?"

"A cook—a very good one."

"Would you be surprised to hear of his being in England three years ago?"

"Not at all," Wing answered assuredly. "Many Chinamen come here. And he could easily have arrived on some ship trading from China or Burma."

"In which case, if he were still here, are there ways one could get to hear of him?"

The very faintest ghost of a smile showed itself in the wrinkles about the Chinaman's eyes as he inclined his head a little.

"Because if we want to get to the bottom of these two murders, I believe that Chuh Fen might be able to throw light on the whole episode," the detective persisted.

Taking the initiative, Lorrimore turned to his servant and addressed him in some strange tongue in which Wing at once responded. For some minutes, they talked together volubly before the doctor looked round at Scarterfield.

"Wing says that if Chuh Fen was in London three years ago, he can find out how long he was there, whence he came, and where he went if anywhere. I gather that there's a sort of freemasonry amongst these men—naturally, they seek each other out in strange lands, and there are places to which a Chinaman resorts if he happens to land in England."

"There is one other thing, of course" said Scarterfield. "If Chuh Fen is still in England—as he may be—can your man find him?"

Wing's smooth countenance, on hearing this, showed some sign of animation. Instead of replying to the detective, he again addressed his master in the foreign tongue. Lorrimore nodded and turned to Scarterfield with a slightly cynical smile.

"He says that if Chuh Fen is anywhere in England then he can lay hands on him in principle," said Lorrimore. "But he adds that it might not be convenient to Chuh Fen to come into the full light of day at present: he may have reasons of his own for desiring strict privacy."

"Understood," said Scarterfield, equably. "All right, doctor— if Mr. Wing here can unearth Mr. Chuh Fen, and that mysterious gentleman can give me a lead, I will leave his privacy as I found it. In addition, all expenses will be defrayed and there'll be a handsome remuneration on completion of the task."

"You can leave it to him," said Lorrimore. "If there's news to be had of Chuh Fen, Wing will get it."

"Good," said Scarterfield, with evident relish. "I like to see a bit of progress. But while I'm here, and we're all at business, let us turn our attention to this fugitive tobacco box that disappeared during the time of Salter Quick's interest . . ."

Instinctively, I turned to Mr. Cazalette, who seemed in two minds about repeating what he'd told me earlier. With a slight nod of the head, I gave it to be known that I thought he should.

Nodding himself, he cleared his voice, then told the story of the tobacco box, and of his pocket-book, for the second time in quick succession. It came as a surprise to all there but myself, and I saw that Mr. Raven in particular was much perturbed by the story of the theft that morning. I knew what he was thinking —that criminals were much too close at hand for his liking. He cut in now and then with a question, while the detective listened in grim, absorbed silence. As he neared the end of his discourse, Mr. Cazalette added weight to it. From the depths of his breast pocket, he took out the photographic print.

The rest of us watched Scarterfield as he studied the image which Mr. Cazalette and I had exercised our brains over prior to dinner. He seemed to get no more information from a long perusal of it than we had earlier, and finally slid it back across the table, expressing evident frustration. It was then, with no less curiosity, that Miss Raven picked the photograph up.

"Aye," said Mr. Cazalette. "Let the lassie look at it! Maybe a woman's brains is more use than a man's is."

"Often," said the detective. "And if Miss Raven can make anything of that, then I would be greatly in her debt."

For her own part, Miss Raven looked up from the photograph and over at Scarterfield.

"Were I to hazard a guess, I'd say that this is a rough outline of the churchyard that Salter Quick was searching for. These outer lines may be the wall," she said, looking down again, and tracing a finger over the evidence. "While these little marks may show the situation of the Netherfield graves. As for that cross in the corner—if such it is—perhaps that marks the spot where something is buried."

Enthused by the young woman's speculations, the detective picked up the photograph once more. "Upon my word, I shouldn't wonder—that could very well be true!"

"Except, there isn't anybody of the name of Netherfield buried between Alnmouth and Budle Bay," remarked Mr. Cazalette solemnly.

The police inspector nodded in agreement. "I can vouch for that. Our exhaustive inquiry reached the very same conclusion."

Scarterfield appeared less ready to dismiss the idea. "Unless Salter Quick was slightly wayward in his calculations. What we do know is that the Netherfield who was with him on the *Elizabeth Robinson* hailed from Blyth, in this self same county. That's why I'm going to Blyth myself tomorrow to find out if there are any Netherfields buried about there. Personally, I believe Miss Raven's hit the nail on the head—this is a rough chart of a spot Salter Quick wanted to find, where something is no doubt hidden. And judging from the fact that two men have been murdered for the secret of it—it's something of tremendous value."

"Buried treasure," murmured Mr. Cazalette, enthralled by the possibility.

Drawing himself up in his chair, Scarterfield looked about the table. "But now, before we part, let us see where we've got to. I, for myself, have drawn five distinct conclusions about this affair:

"*First*—That the Quicks, Noah and Salter, were in possession of a secret, which was probably connected with their shipmate of the *Elizabeth Robinson*.

"*Second*—That certain men knew the Quicks to be in possession of that secret and murdered both to get hold of it.

"*Third*—That they failed to get it from either Noah or Salter.

"*Fourth*—That Mr. Cazalette's zeal about the tobacco box, publicly expressed, put the criminals on a new scent, and that they stole both the tobacco box and Mr. Cazalette's pocket-book in pursuance of it.

"*Fifth*—That the criminals are—or were very recently—still in this vicinity.

"So," he continued, looking round him, "the thing appears to be narrowing. Let Mr. Wing here procure news of Chuh Fen while I follow up on the Netherfield lead. One way or another, I'm optimistic of a breakthrough—I think we shall track these fellows yet."

"You've not said anything about the handkerchief that I found," observed Mr. Cazalette. "There's a clue, surely."

Scarterfield gave a nod of acknowledgement. "But difficult to follow up on, sir. Now if we could trace the owner of the hand-kerchief, and find where he gets his washing done, that would put a different complexion on the matter. But we'll not lose sight of it, Mr. Cazalette—you have my word on that—only there are more important clues to go on in the meantime."

The two police officials went away with Dr. Lorrimore, all in deep converse, while the four of us who were left behind endeavoured to settle our minds for the repose of the night. But I saw that Mr. Raven had been upset by the recent talk. Indeed, he had got it firmly fixed in his consciousness that the murderer of Salter Quick was, as it were, in our very midst.

"How do I know that the guilty man isn't one of my own servants?" he murmured ominously as Mr. Cazalette and I took up our candles. "There are six men in the house—all essentially strangers to me—and several employed outside whose inner lives are no more clear."

Mr. Cazalette shook his head firmly in the flickering candlelight. "Nay, Raven. The murderer may be within bow-shot, but he's none o' yours, to be sure. This is no ordinary affair, and no ordinary men lie at the bottom of it."

A short while later, as we went along one of the upstairs passages, Mr. Cazalette gave a censorious shake of the head. "Raven'll be doubting the *bona fides* of his own footmen and garden lads next. Mark my words, this mystery's architects exist elsewhere."

"I shouldn't doubt that," I told him.

"Aye—and I'm wondering if it was well to let yon Chinese fellow into all of this," he muttered significantly.

"Lorrimore answers for him," said I.

"And who answers for Lorrimore?" he demanded. " If you ask me, he knows more than he's letting on, and the same is true of that Wing character to boot."

However Mr. Raven's nerves may have been wrung, nothing untoward occurred at Ravensdene Court in the following days. Indeed, had it not been for the visit of the inspector and Scarterfield, and the ensuing speculations, daily life would have been regular to the point of monotony. We were all engaged in our respective avocations—Mr. Cazalette with his coins and medals; I with my books and papers; Miss Raven with her flowers and golf; and Mr. Raven with his steward, gardeners, and various potterings about the estate.

Mr. Raven and Mr. Cazalette made common cause of an afternoon; they were of that period of life—despite the gulf of twenty years between them—when lounging in comfortable chairs under old cedar trees on a sunlit lawn is preferable to active exercise. Miss Raven and I being younger, found our diversion in golf and in occasional explorations of the surrounding countryside. She had a touch of the nomadic instinct in her—as had I—and the surrounding neighbourhood was, broadly speaking, new to us both. So it was we began to find great pleasure in setting out on some excursion as soon as lunch was over and prolonging our wanderings until the falling shadows warned us that it was time to head back.

We heard nothing of Scarterfield, nor of Wing, for some days after the consultation in Mr. Raven's dining room. Then, as we were breakfasting one morning, the post bag was brought in, and Mr. Raven handed me a letter whose envelope bore a Blyth postmark. I guessed that it was from the detective, and began to wonder what on earth had made him write to me.

Opening the envelope with a butter knife, I soon had my answer:

NORTH SEA HOTEL,
BLYTH, NORTHUMBERLAND
April 23, 1912

Dear Sir,

You will remember that when we were discussing matters the other night round Mr. Raven's table, I mentioned that I intended visiting this town in order to launch further inquiries. I have now been here two days, and have made some very curious discoveries, it has to be said. For that same reason, I am writing to ask if you could so far oblige me as to join me here for a day or two and aid these investigations? The fact is, I want your assistance as I understand that you are an expert in deciphering documents and the like, and I have come across certain things here which are beyond me. If you could spare me even a few hours of your valuable time that would put me under great obligations to you.

Yours truly,
THOMAS SCARTERFIELD

. . .

I read the letter twice over before handing it to Mr. Raven. Its perusal seemed to excite him.

"Bless me!" he exclaimed. "How very extraordinary! What strange mysteries we seem to be living amongst? You'll go, of course, Middlebrook?"

"You think I should?" I asked.

"Oh, certainly, certainly!" he said with emphasis. "If any of us can do anything to solve this strange problem, I think we should. Of course, one hasn't the faintest idea what it is that the man wants. But from what I observed of him the other evening, I should say that Scarterfield is a very clever fellow."

"Scarterfield has made some discoveries at Blyth," I remarked, glancing at Miss Raven and at Mr. Cazalette, who were both manifesting great curiosity, "He wants me to go over there and help him—to elucidate something, I think—but what it is, I have no idea."

"Oh, of course, you must go!" exclaimed Miss Raven. "How exciting! Mr. Cazalette, aren't you jealous?"

"No, but I am curious," he answered readily, eyeing the letter which I had just passed to him. "Didn't I tell all of you, all along, that there'd be more in this business than met the eye? It's a strange fact, but in affairs of this sort there's often strong circumstantial evidence ready to be picked up if you pursue it long and hard enough. And in this case it's almost next door, for Blyth's a town that's not so far away."

Far away or near away, it took me some hours to get to Blyth, for I had to drive to Alnwick, and later change at Morpeth, and then again at Newsham. But there I was at last, in the middle of the afternoon, and there on the platform was the detective to greet me.

"I got your telegram, Mr. Middlebrook," he remarked as we walked away from the station, "and I've booked you the most comfortable room I could get in the hotel, which is a nice quiet house where we'll be able to talk in privacy. Barring you and myself there's nobody stopping in it, except a few commercial travellers, and they have their own quarters. Out of interest, have you lunched on the way?"

"While I waited at Morpeth," I answered.

"Good," he said, "Then we'll just get into a corner of the smoking room and have a quiet glass over a cigar, and I'll tell you what I've made out here. A very strange and queer tale it is, and one that's worth hearing, whether it really has to do with our affair or no."

"You're not sure that it has?" I asked.

"I'm as sure as I may be," he replied, "but there's still a gulf between extreme probability and absolute certainty that's a bit wider than the unthinking reckon for. However, here we are— let's get ourselves comfortable. I will share what I now know."

Scarterfield's idea of comfort was to dispose himself in the easiest of chairs in the quietest of corners with a whisky and soda in one hand and a fine cigars in the other. This sort of thing was evidently regarded by him as a proper relaxation from his severe mental labours. I had no objection to it myself after four hours slow travelling—yet I confess I felt keenly impatient as he mixed our drinks, lighted his cigar, and settled down at my elbow.

"Now," he said confidentially, "I'll set it all out in order— what I've found out since I came here two days ago. To begin with, I went to the likeliest people for news, but nobody knew anything of any man named William Netherfield who'd belonged to this town, past or present. However, the same could not be said of a man called Netherfield Baxter who used to be much in evidence here some years ago.

"Netherfield Baxter," I repeated. "Not a name to be readily forgotten."

Scarterfield shook his head grimly. "He's not forgotten by a long chalk."

"Right," I said, intrigued by this sober preface. "Then please tell me more."

"Netherfield Baxter was the only child of an old tradesman of this town, whose wife died when Netherfield was a mere boy, and who died himself when his son was only seventeen years of age. Old Baxter was a remarkably foolish man. He left all he had to this lad—some twelve thousand pounds—in such a fashion that he came into absolute, uncontrolled possession of it on attaining his twenty-first birthday. Now you can imagine what happened next! With nobody to restrain him or give him a word in season—or a hearty kicking, which would have been more to the purpose!—the young fellow went to rack and ruin. Horses, cards, champagne. The twelve thousand began to melt like wax in a fire.

"Young Baxter carried on longer than was expected, for now and then he had luck on the race-course; won a good deal once on the big race at Newcastle—what they call the Pitman's Darby. But all of it went in due course, and by the beginning of the year 1904—bear the date in mind, Mr. Middlebrook—Netherfield Baxter was just about on his last legs. That said, he still had good clothes—and a fine-looking fellow he was said to be—along with decent lodgings. But in spring 1904, he was living on the proceeds of chance betting, and in May of that year he disappeared in sudden fashion, without saying a word to anybody, and since then nobody hereabouts has ever seen or heard a word from him."

Scarterfield paused meaningfully, as if to ask what I thought of it. A good deal, as it happened.

"A very interesting bit of life-drama, Scarterfield," said I. "And there have been far stranger things than for this Netherfield Baxter of Blyth to turn out to be the William Netherfield of the *Elizabeth Robinson*. Which begs the obvious question: have you hit on anything that connects the two?"

"Not as yet," he answered. "And in truth, I doubt that I shall. Nobody in this place has heard of Netherfield Baxter since he walked out of his lodging one evening and clean vanished, and nor are any of them anxious to hear of him."

"But you have more to tell," I said hopefully.

"Oh, much more!" he grinned. "We're less than halfway through the surface matters. Now in May 1904, the Old Alliance Bank here had been placed in charge of a temporary manager in consequence of the regular manager's long-continued illness. This temporary manager was a chap named Lester—John Martindale Lester—who had come here from a branch of the same bank at Hexham. This Lester chap was greatly given to going about on a motorcycle and was always tearing about the country. Then one evening, careering round a sharp corner, somewhere just outside the town, he ran full tilt into a cart that carried no tail-light and broke his neck."

"Well?" said I.

"So John Martindale Lester was killed about the beginning of the first week in May 1904. It was three or four days later that Netherfield Baxter cleared out. I've been careful in my conversations with the town folk—officials, mostly—not to connect Lester's death with Baxter's departure. Nonetheless, I'm certain there was a connection. Baxter fled because he knew that Lester's sudden death would lead to an examination of things at the Old Alliance Bank."

"Ah!" said I. "And was this examination forthcoming?"

"Indeed it was," the inspector answered. "And some nice revelations there were too. To begin with, there was a cash deficiency—not a heavy one, but quite heavy enough to warrant suspicion. In addition to that, certain jewels were missing, which had been deposited with the bankers for security by a lady in this neighbourhood, and worth some thousands of pounds. Two chests of plate were also gone which had been placed with the bank some years before by the executors of the will of the late Lord Forestburne, to be kept there till the coming of age of his heir. Altogether, Mr. John Martindale Lester and his accomplices had helped themselves very freely to things in the vaults and the strongroom."

"Have you found out if Netherfield Baxter and the temporary bank manager were acquainted?" I asked.

"No—that's a matter I've carefully refrained from inquiring into," answered Scarterfield. "So far, no one has mentioned their acquaintanceship or association to me, and I haven't suggested it, for I don't want to raise suspicions."

"But what is thought in the town about Lester and the valuables?" I inquired. "They must have some working theory?"

"Oh, of course, they have," he replied. "The theory is that Lester had accomplices in London, that he shipped these valuables off there, and that when his accomplices heard of his sudden death they simply held their tongues. But my notion is that the only accomplice Lester had was our friend Netherfield Baxter."

"You've some ground?" I asked.

"Yes," said Scarterfield, "and I'm now coming to the reason of my sending for you, Mr. Middlebrook. I told you that this fellow Baxter had a decent lodging in the town. Well, I made it my business to go there yesterday morning, and finding that the landlady was a sensible woman, and likely to keep a quiet tongue, I asked her some questions. In that way I found out that Baxter had left various matters behind him, which she still had in her possession. Clothes, books (he was evidently a chap for reading, and of superior education), papers, and the like.

"I got her to let me have a sight of them, and amongst the papers I found two, which seem to me to have been written hundreds of years ago and to be lists with names and figures on them. My impression is that Lester found them in those chests of plate, couldn't make them out, and gave them to Netherfield Baxter as being a better educated man. Baxter did well at school and could read and write two or three languages. Well now I persuaded the landlady to lend me these documents for a day or two, and I've got them in my room upstairs, safely under lock and key. I'll fetch them down presently and you shall see if you can decipher them—very old they are, and the writing crabbed and queer—but Lord bless you, the ink's as black as jet!"

"Scarterfield," said I, excitedly. "It strikes me that you've hit on a veritable discovery. Supposing this stolen stuff is hidden somewhere about? Supposing Netherfield Baxter knew exactly where, and that he's the William Netherfield of the *Elizabeth Robinson*? Supposing that he let the Quicks into the secret? Supposing—but, bless me! there are a hundred things one can suppose! Anyhow, I believe we're onto something."

"I've been supposing a great deal myself since yesterday morning, as you'd expect," answered the detective. "Now I'll fetch down these documents and we can see if any of these suppositions carry any weight."

He went away, and while he was absent I stood at the window of the smoking room, looking out on the life of the little town. There across the street, immediately in front of the hotel, was the bank of which Scarterfield had been telling me. It was an old-fashioned, grey-walled, red-roofed place, the outer door of which was just then being closed for the day by a white-whiskered old porter. Was it possible—could it really be—that the story which had recently ended in a double murder had begun in that quiet-looking house, through the criminality of an untrustworthy employee? But did I say ended? Nay, for all I knew the murder of the Quicks was only an episode, a chapter in a far greater story that was still to reach its definite conclusion. Thrilled by this possibility, I waited to see what revelations awaited me next.

❧ 16 ❧

On his return, Scarterfield drew forth from a big envelope, and placed in my hands, two folded pieces of old, time-yellowed parchment. Until that moment I had not thought much about the reason of my presence at Blyth —I had, at any rate, thought no more than that Scarterfield had merely come across some writing which he found it hard to decipher. But one glance at the documents showed me that he had accidentally come across a really important find, and within another moment, I was deeply engrossed. The detective sat silently watching me, nodding once or twice when I looked up at him, as if to imply that he had felt sure of the importance of these papers. Presently, laying them on the table between us, I sought to put them in context:

"Scarterfield, are you at all up on the history of your own country?"

"Couldn't say that I am, Mr. Middlebrook," he answered with a shake of his head. "Not beyond what a lad learns at school— and I dare say I've forgotten a lot of that in the meantime. My job, you see, has always been with the hard facts of the actual present."

"But you're familiar with certain notable episodes," I

suggested. "You know, for instance, that when the religious houses were suppressed—abbeys, priories, and convents—in the reign of Henry the Eighth, a great deal of their plate and jewels were confiscated?"

"Oh, I've heard that!" he admitted. "Nice haul the old chap got, too, I'm given to understand."

"He didn't get it all," said I. "A great deal of the monastic plate simply disappeared. It used to be said that a lot of it was hidden away or buried by its owners. However, it's much more likely that it was stolen by the greedy folk of the neighbourhood. Anyway, while a great deal was certainly sent by the commissioners to the king's treasury in London, a lot more—especially in out-of-the-way places and districts—just disappeared and was never heard of again. Up here in the North of England that was very often the case. All this is merely a preface to what I'm going to tell you. Have you the least idea of what these documents are?"

"No," he replied. "Unless they're lists of something—I did make out that they might be by the way the words and figures are arranged. Inventories or some such like."

"They are inventories," I applauded him. "Both written in crabbed caligraphy, but easy enough to read if you're acquainted with sixteenth century penmanship, spelling and abbreviations. Look at the first one. It is here described as an inventory of all the jewels, plate, and valuables appertaining to the Abbey of Forestburne. It was made in the year 1536, which means that this abbey was one of the smaller houses that came under the £200 limit and was accordingly suppressed in the year just mentioned. Now look at the second one. It is also an inventory of jewels and plate, made in the same year, this time belonging to the Priory of Mellerton. But although both of these houses were of the smaller sort, it is quite evident from a cursory glance that they were pretty rich in material terms"

"Worth a good deal, eh?" Scarterfield asked.

"A great deal!" I answered, "if it's still in existence. But let me read you a few of the items set down here, with their weight in ounces specified. A chalice, twenty-eight ounces. Another chalice, thirty-six ounces. A mazer, forty-seven ounces. One pair candlesticks, fifty-two ounces. A great cross, seventy-two ounces. Three tablets of proper gold work, eighty-five ounces in total. And so on and so on!—a very nice collection, considering that these are only a few items I've chosen at random out of some seventy or eighty altogether. But we can easily reckon up the total weight—indeed, it's already reckoned up at the foot of each inventory. At Forestburne, there was a sum total of two thousand, two hundred and thirty-eight ounces of plate. At Mellerton, one thousand eight hundred and seventy ounces. So these two inventories, taken together, represent a mass of about four thousand ounces. Worth laying your hands on in the sixteenth century, and even more so today!"

"And in the main, it would be—what?" asked Scarterfield. "Gold, silver?"

"Some of it gold, some silver, a good deal of it silver-gilt," I told him.

"Four thousand ounces of the stuff!" he exclaimed. "Good Lord! So what do you make of it in relation to our own mystery?"

"I would surmise that this plate, originally church property, came into the hands of the late Lord Forestburne. In all likelihood, his family had retained possession of it for the best part of four centuries. This being the case, he'd had it deposited it with his bankers across the way. He may, indeed, not have known what was in the chests—again, he may have known. Now I take it that the dishonest temporary manager you told me about, having examined them in turn, decided to appropriate their valuable contents, and enlisted the services of Netherfield Baxter for this nefarious purpose. These inventories would have been found in the chests—one in each—and Baxter must have kept them out of sheer curiosity, what with him being a fellow of some education. As for the plate itself, I think that he and his associate must have hidden it somewhere. Based on what we know so far, Salter Quick must have thought so too."

Scarterfield clapped his hand on the table.

"That's it!" he exclaimed. "Hanged if I don't think that myself! It's my opinion that this Netherfield Baxter, after fleeing here, came into touch with the Quicks and told 'em the secret of this stolen plate. He was, I'm sure, the same Netherfield of that ship the brothers were sailing on. I think we may safely bet on it that Salter Quick was looking for this hidden treasure!"

"As was somebody else," said I. "That same person who murdered Quick in cold blood."

"And what's the next thing to do in your opinion, Mr. Middlebrook, based on this working theory?"

"If I were you, I should begin by taking two people into your confidence—the current director of the bank, and the present Lord Forestburne."

Scarterfield offered a resounding nod in agreement. "I'll see them both first thing tomorrow morning. Would you be so good as to go with me? You can explain the nature of these old papers far better than I."

After dinner, on retiring to my room, I speculated some more on the stolen plate. There were collectors, English and American, who would cheerfully give vast sums for pre-Reformation sacramental vessels. Transactions of this kind, I fancied, must have been in the minds of the two thieves. And yet there were features of the whole affair which still puzzled me— not least the fact that church property should have remained so long in the Forestburne family without being brought into the light of day. I hoped that our inquiries next morning would bring some information on that point.

But we got no information—at least, none of any consequence. All that was known by the authorities at the bank was that the late Lord Forestburne had deposited two chests of plate with them years before, with instructions that they were to remain in the bank's custody until his son succeeded him. Even then they were not to be opened unless the son had already come of age. The bank people had no knowledge of the precise contents of the chests—all they knew was that they contained plate. As for the present Lord Forestburne, he knew nothing except that his father's mysterious deposit had been burgled by a dishonest custodian. As for the chief authority at the bank, a crusty and self-sufficient old gentleman, he scorned the notion that the inventories had anything to do with the rifled Forestburne chests, or that the family had ever been in possession of goods obtained by sacrilege.

"Preposterous!" said he, with a sniff of contempt. "What the chests contained was superfluous family plate, and nothing more than that. As for these documents, that fellow Baxter, in spite of his loose manner of living, was inclined to a bit of scholarship. He probably picked up these parchments in some bookseller's shop in Durham or Newcastle. I don't believe they've anything to do with Lord Forestburne's stolen property, and I advise you both not to waste time in running after mare's nests."

Scarterfield and I got ourselves out of this starchy person's presence and confided to each other our private opinions of him and his intelligence. For us both, the theory which we had already set up was unassailable. We tried to reduce it to strict and formal precision as we ate our lunch in a quiet corner of the hotel coffee room, prior to parting.

"Returning to the *Elizabeth Robinson*," said I, "we know that whatever happened to the rest of those on board, three men at any rate saved their lives—Noah Quick, Salter Quick and the Chinese cook, whose exact name we've forgotten, but one of whose patronymics was Chuh. Some years later, Chuh turns up at Lloyds of London and asks a question about the vanished ship. Around the same time, Noah Quick materialises at Devonport, soon to be joined by his brother. And presently Salter is up on the Northumbrian coast, professing great anxiety to find a churchyard wherein are graves with the name Netherfield engraved upon them. Now we know what happened to Salter

Quick, and we also know what happened to Noah Quick. But now I'm wondering if something else had happened before that?"

"And would you care to hazard a guess?" Scarterfield prompted me.

Taking up the invitation, I leaned nearer to him across the little table at which we sat. "I'm wondering if Noah and Salter had murdered this Netherfield Baxter before they themselves were murdered. There have been known such cases, where a secret is shared by five or six men, and in which murder after murder occurs until the secret is only held by one or two of them. A half-share in a thing is worth more than one-sixth, Scarterfield. And a secret of one is far more valuable than a secret shared with three."

"Well," he said, "if that's so, there were are least two men concerned in putting the Quicks away. For Noah was finished off on the same night that saw Salter finished—and there was four hundred miles distance between the scenes of their respective murders. The man who killed Noah was not the man who killed Salter, to be sure."

"Of course," I agreed. "We've always known there were two. There may be more—a whole gang of them—and all remarkably clever fellows. But I'm sure that the desire to recover this hidden treasure prompted both killings. That said, there are a good many things that still puzzle me."

"Such as what?" Scarterfield asked.

"If the men who murdered Noah and Salter Quick were in possession of the secret as well, why did they rip their clothes to pieces? And why later did somebody steal that tobacco box from under the very noses of the police?"

Scarterfield looked at me pensively. "And were you at the inquest yourself?"

"I was there," said I. "So were most people of the neighbour-hood—as many as could get into the room, anyway. When the proceedings were over, men were crowding about the table on which Quick's things had been laid out for exhibition to the coroner and the jury. Little wonder that the theft passed unnoticed, given the large melee."

Before Scarterfield could reply, one of the hotel servants came into the coffee-room and made for our table.

"There's a man in the hall asking for Mr. Scarterfield," he announced. "Looks like a seafaring man, sir. He says Mrs. Ormthwaite told him he'd find you here."

"The woman with whom Baxter used to lodge," said Scarterfield, in a quick aside to me. "Come along, Mr. Middlebrook—let's see what this sailor has to say."

❧ 17 ❧

It needed but one glance at Scarterfield's visitor to assure me that he was a person who was used to the sea. There was the suggestion of salt water and strong winds all over him, from his grizzled hair and beard to his big, brawny hands and square set build. He looked the sort of man who all his life had been looking out across wide stretches of ocean and battling with the forces of Nature in her roughest moods. Just then there was questioning in his keen blue eyes—he was obviously wondering, with all the native suspicion of a simple soul, what Scarterfield might be after.

"You're asking for me?" said the detective.

The man glanced from one to the other of us; then jerked a big thumb in the direction of some region beyond the open door.

"Mrs. Ormthwaite," he said, bending a little towards Scarterfield. "She said as how there was a gentleman stopping in this here house as was making inquiries about Netherfield Baxter, so I thought to come along."

Without another word, Scarterfield turned towards the door of the smoking room, motioning his visitor to follow. We all went into the corner wherein, on the previous afternoon,

Scarterfield had told me of his investigations and discoveries. Evidently I was now to hear more. But Scarterfield asked for no further information until he had provided our companion with refreshment in the shape of a glass of rum and a cigar.

"What's your name, then?" the detective inquired finally.

"Solomon Fish," came the prompt reply.

"Blyth man, no doubt," suggested Scarterfield.

"Born and bred, master," Fish answered. "And lived here always—'cepting when I been away at sea. But whether north or south, east or west, I always make for the old spot when I'm back on dry land after a spell of journeying."

"So you knew Netherfield Baxter?" asked Scarterfield.

Fish waved his cigar.

"As a baby, a boy, an' a young man," he declared freely. "Cut many a toy boat for him at one stage, taught him to fish at another, went sailing with him in a bit of a yawl that he had when he was growed up. Yes, sir – I knew him all right!"

"Quite so," said Scarterfield. "And when did you see him last, can you tell me?"

Fish, to my surprise, gave a laugh that betokened incredulity and a great sense of puzzlement.

"That's just it, master! I asks you—and this other gent— can a man trust his own eyes and ears when it comes to such matters?"

"I've always trusted mine," answered Scarterfield.

"Same here," Fish replied. "But now I ain't so mortal sure. Cause according to my eyes, and according to my ears, I seen and heard Netherfield Baxter not three weeks ago!"

He brought down his big hand on the table with a hearty smack as he spoke this last word. The sound of it was followed by a dead silence in which Scarterfield and I exchanged freighted glances. Fish picked up his tumbler, took a gulp at its contents, and then set it down with renewed emphasis.

"Gospel truth!" he said forcefully.

"You're sure?" asked Scarterfield.

Fish nodded. "If my eyes and ears are to be trusted. Only he said as how he wasn't himself!

That was the queerest thing of all. Wouldn't hear of me knowing him."

"You mean that the man you took for Baxter said you were mistaken?" suggested Scarterfield.

"You puts it very plain, master," assented Fish. "But if the man I refers to wasn't Netherfield Baxter, then I've no more eyes than this here cigar, and no more ears than that glass!"

"And where was this?" the detective continued.

"Hull," replied Fish. "Three weeks ago come Friday."

"Under what circumstances?" Scarterfield persisted.

"Well, you see, I landed at Hull from my last voyage—been out East and back with a trading vessel what belongs to Hull owners. And before coming home here to Blyth, I knocked about a day or two in that port with an old messmate o' mine that I chanced to meet. Now then, one morning, the two of us turns into a certain old-fashioned place there is in Hull, in a bit of an alley off the High Street, that goes by the name of the Goose and Crane. As snug a spot as you'll find in any shipping town in this here country."

"I've seen it from outside, Fish," I interjected. "A fine old front—half timber."

"That's it, guv'nor—and as pleasant inside as it's remarkable outside," he said. "Well, my mate and me we goes in there for a morning glass, and into a room where you'll find some interesting folk about that time o' day. There's a sign on the door o' that room, gentlemen, what reads 'For Master Mariners Only,' but it's an old piece of work, and you don't want to take no heed of it—me and Shanks we ain't master mariners, though we may look it from a distance.

"Well, now we gets our glasses, and our cigars, and we sits down in a quiet corner to enjoy ourselves and observe what company drops in. Some queer old birds there is comes in to that place, I do assure you, gentlemen, and some strange tales o' seafaring life you can hear. Still, nothing particular struck me that morning until it was getting on for dinnertime, and me an Shanks was thinking o' laying a course for our lodgings. It was then that a man walks in what I'd known since he was knee high to a grasshopper."

"Netherfield Baxter?" asked Scarterfield.

Fish nodded. "Just so."

"It'll be best if you can give us a description of this man."

Hearing the detective's request, our visitor seemed to pull his mental faculties together. He took another pull at his glass and several at his cigar.

"Well," he said, "t'aint much in my line, but I can give a general idea. A tallish, good-looking chap, as the women 'ud call handsome, sort of rakish fellow, you understand. Dressed very smart: blue serge suit, straw hat, and brown boots—polished and shining. Quite the swell, as Netherfield always was, even when he'd got through his money. The biggest change in him was that he'd grown a beard and moustache since I saw him last."

"What colour?" asked Scarterfield.

"What you might call a golden-brown," replied Fish. "And it suited him well enough."

Scarterfield drew out his pocket-book and produced a slightly-faded photograph—that of a certain good-looking young man, taken in company with a fox-terrier.

"Is that Baxter?" he asked.

"Aye!—as he was years ago," Fish answered. "But you'd still recognize him from that, but for the new beard and moustache."

"And was he alone?"

"No," replied Fish. "He'd two other men with him. One was a chap about his own age, as smart as he was, and dressed similar. T'other was an older man in his shirt sleeves—seemed to me he'd brought Baxter and his friend across from some shop or other to stand 'em a drink. Anyways, he did call for drinks— whisky and soda—and the three o' them stood together talking. And as soon as I heard Baxter's voice, I was dead sure about him—he'd always a highish voice, talked as gentlemen talks, ye see."

"What were these three talking about?" asked Scarterfield.

"Far as I could make out about ship's fittings," answered Fish. "Something 'o that sort, anyway, but I didn't take much notice o' their talk; I was too much taken up watching Baxter and growing more certain every minute. I didn't see no great change in him, 'cept for the beard, and one other alteration."

"What was that?" Scarterfield asked.

"A scar on his left cheek," replied Fish. "What begun underneath his beard, covered most of it, and went up to his cheekbone. That's been knife's work!' thinks I to myself. 'You've had your cheek laid open with a knife, my lad, somewhere and somehow!' Struck me then, he must have grown a beard to hide it."

"Very likely," assented Scarterfield. "And what happened next? Did you approach this individual?"

"I waited and watched," continued Fish. "I'm one as has been trained to use his eyes. Now, I see two or three little things about this man as I remembered about Baxter. There was a way he had of chucking up his chin—there it was! Another of playing with his watch-chain when he talked—it was there too! And of slapping his leg with his walking stick, which was also plain in evidence. 'Jim!' I says to my mate, 'if that ain't a man I used to know, I'm a Dutchman!' And so when the three of 'em sets down their glasses and turns to the door, I jumps up and makes for my man, holding out a hand to him.

"'Morning, Mr. Baxter!' says I. 'It's a long time since I had the pleasure o' seeing you, sir!' Then he turns and gives me a hard, keen look—not taken aback, mind you, but searching-like. 'You're mistaken, my friend,' he says, pleasant enough. 'You're taking me for somebody else.' 'What!' says I, all of a heap. 'Ain't you Mr. Netherfield Baxter, what I used to know at Blyth, away up North?' 'That I'm certainly not,' says he, as cool as you like. 'Then I ax your pardon, sir,' says I, 'and all I can say is that I never seen two gentlemen so much alike in all my born days, and hoping no offence.' 'None at all!' says he, as pleasant as might be. 'They say everybody has a double.' And at that he gives me a polite nod, and out he goes with his pals, and I turns back to Shanks. 'Jim!' says I. 'Don't let me ever trust my eyes and ears no more!" 'Stow all that!' says Jim, 'I've been in that case more than once. Wherever there's a man, there's another that's as like him as two peas is like each other. Let's go home to dinner,' he says. So we went off to the lodgings, and at first I was sure I'd been mistaken. But with every day that's passed since then, I've been less and less sure."

"You really think that man was Netherfield Baxter!" Scarterfield asked him.

"Certain of it, master!" declared Fish. "I've had time to think it over, and to reckon it all up, and now I'm sure it was him—only he wasn't going to let on."

"And did you see any more of him in Hull?"

""Yes, I did," answered Fish. "I saw him again that very night in the smoking-room of the Cross Keys. Shanks and me had no sooner sat us down, and taken an observation , when I sees the same man in the far corner, with the other smart-dressed man sat across from him. And with 'em there was somebody else that I certainly didn't expect to see in that place."

"Who?" asked Scarterfield.

"A Chinaman," Fish answered, "but not of the common sort that you'll see by the score down in Limehouse way, or in Liverpool or Cardiff. Lord bless you, this here chap was smarter dressed than t'other two! Swell-made dark clothes, gold-handled umbrella, kid gloves on his blooming hands, and a silk top-hat to top it off!"

"Did the man you take to be Baxter look at you at all?" asked Scarterfield.

"Never showed a sign of it!" declared Fish. "Him and t'other passed us on their way to the door, but he took no notice."

"See him again anywhere?" inquired Scarterfield.

"No, I didn't" replied Fish. "I left Hull early next morning, and went to see relatives o' mine at South Shields. Only came home a day or two since, and happened to be passing the time o' day with widow Ormthwaite this morning, when she told me about your inquiries, so I come along here to see you."

Scarterfield nodded. "Well, needless to say, Mr Fish, I'm most grateful for your submission."

After taking the man's address, and other details, Solomon Fish was free to leave our table.

As soon as he'd made his exit, the detective turned to me.

"There!" he said. "What d'you think of that, Mr. Middlebrook?"

"I could ask the same of you," I answered.

"That Netherfield Baxter is alive and well and clearly up to something," he commented. "And I'd give a good deal to know who that Chinaman is who was with him. But there's ways of finding out, which is why I'm bound for Hull at the earliest opportunity. You'll come with me, Mr. Middlebrook—I dare say you'd welcome some answers."

Such an idea had never entered my head, but I made up my mind readily. "I will, Mr Scarterfield. I should like to see this through."

✺ 18 ✺

There were good reasons—other than the desire to follow this business to whatever end it might come—which induced me to consent to the detective's suggestion. I knew the city of Hull well enough, having spent an annual holiday there with relatives in my very youthful days, and had vivid recollections of the place.

Even then, they had begun to pull Hull to pieces, laying out fine new streets and open spaces where there had been old-fashioned, narrow alleys and slum dwellings. Happily now, there was still the old Hull of the ancient High Street, and the Market Place, and the older docks, wharves, and quaysides. It had been amongst these survivals of antiquity that I had loved to wander as a boy, as there was a peculiar smell of the sea in Hull, and an atmosphere of seafaring life that I have never met with elsewhere, neither in Wapping nor in Bristol, in Southampton nor in Liverpool. One felt in Hull that one was already half-way to Bergen or Stockholm or Riga. Indeed, there was something of North Europe about you as soon as you crossed the bridge at the top of Whitefriargate and caught sight of the masts and funnels, and huge sheds bursting with foreign merchandise. And I had a sudden half-sentimental desire to see the old seaport again, and experience its resolute charms once more.

Going southward by way of Newcastle and York, we got to Hull that night, late—too late to do more than eat our suppers and go to bed at the Station Hotel. And we took things leisurely next morning, breakfasting late and strolling through the older part of the town before approaching the Goose and Crane as noon drew near.

We had a specific aim in selecting this time and place. Fish had told us that the man whom he'd seen in company with Baxter had entered the old inn in his shirt-sleeves and without his hat. He was therefore probably some neighbouring shop or store-keeper, and in the habit of turning into the ancient hostelry for a drink about noontime. Such, at least, was the man that Scarterfield hoped to encounter.

Although, I had often seen the street front of the Goose and Crane as a boy, I had never passed its portals. Now, on entering it, we found it to be even more curious inside than it was out. It was a fine relic of Tudor days—a rabbit warren of snug rooms, old furniture, wide chimney places, and tiled floors. If the folk who frequented it had only worn the right sorts of costume, we might easily have thought ourselves back in Elizabethan times. As it was, we easily found the particular room of which Solomon Fish had spoken—there was the door, half open, with its legend on an upper panel in faded gilt letters: "For Master Mariners Only." But as Fish had remarked, that warning had been set up in the old days, and was no longer a strict observance. We went into the room unquestioned by guardians or occupants, and then, after calling for refreshments, sat ourselves down to watch and wait.

There were several men in this quaint old parlour who seemed connected with the sea to one degree or another. Most were thick-set, sturdy, bronzed, branded in solid suits of good blue cloth, and with that faraway look in the eye which stamps the seafarer. Other men there present looked more like ship's chandlers or shipping-agents. We caught stray whiffs of talk relating to the life of the port and the wide North Sea that stretches away from the Humber. And it was as we sifted among these snatches that the man we were looking for, like as not, walked in.

He was a shortish, stiffly-built paunchy man with a beefy face, shrewd eyes, and a bristling, iron-grey moustache. Well-dressed, he sported a fine gold chain and a diamond pin in his cravat. All the same, he was in his shirt sleeves, and without a hat, which marked him out for our special consideration. Seeing him enter, Scarterfield leaned nearer to me.

"That'd be him," he murmured.

"It certainly looks that way,," I answered.

The newcomer, clearly well known from the familiar way in which nods and brief salutations were exchanged, bustled up to the bar, called for a glass of bitter beer, and helped himself to a crust of bread and a bit of cheese from the provender at his elbow. Leaning one elbow on the counter and munching his snack, he entered into conversation with one or two men near him. Here again, as far as we could follow it, the talk was of seafaring matters. But we did not catch the name of the man in the shirt-sleeves, and when, after he'd finished his refreshment, he nodded to the company and bustled out as quickly as he'd entered, Scarterfield gave me a look and we left the room in his wake.

Our quarry strode down the alley and turned the corner into the old High Street. He was evidently well known here as well and we saw several passers-by exchange greetings with him. Always bustling along, as if he were a man whose time was precious, he presently crossed the narrow roadway and turned into an office, over the window of which was a sign:

Jallanby, Ship Broker

He had only got one foot across the threshold when Scarter-field hurried forward and made his introduction.

"Excuse me, sir," he said politely. "May I have a word with you?"

The man turned around and stared. "Yes?" he answered irritably. "What is it?"

Scarterfield pulled out his pocket-book and produced his official card.

"You'll see who I am from that," he remarked. "This gentleman's a friend of mine—just now giving me some professional help. I take it you're Mr. Jallanby?"

The ship-broker started a little as he glanced at the card and realized Scarterfield's calling.

"Yes, I'm Mr. Jallanby," he answered. "Come inside, gentlemen." He then led the way into a dark, rather dismal and dusty little office, and signed to a clerk who was writing there to go out. "How can I help you, Mr. Scarterfield?" Jallanby finally asked.

"From something we heard only yesterday afternoon, Mr. Jallanby, a long way from here, we believe that one morning about three weeks ago, you were in the Goose and Crane in that very room where we just happened to see you. On that earlier occasion, it was in the company of two smartly dressed men in blue serge suits and straw hats; one of them with a pointed, golden-brown beard. Does that strike a chord with you?"

I was watching the ship-broker's face while Scarterfield spoke, and I saw that deep interest, even suspicion was being aroused in him.

"Bless me!" he exclaimed. "You don't mean to say they're wanted?"

"I mean to say that I need all the information you can provide on the subject," Scarterfield answered. "You do remember that morning, then?"

Jallanby nodded, readily enough. "I went across there with those two several times while they were in town, doing a bit of business. We often dropped in over yonder for a glass before dinner. But I'm surprised that detectives should be inquiring after 'em! To be frank, that comes as quite the shock!"

"Mr. Jallanby," said Scarterfield, "Let me plain with you. At the moment, this is merely a matter of suspicion. I'm not sure of the identity of one of these men—it's but one I want to trace at present—though I should like to know who the other is. But if my man is the man I believe him to be, there's a matter of robbery, and possibly of murder. Now, I'll jog your memory a bit. Do you remember that one morning, as you and these two men were leaving the Goose and Crane, a big seafaring-looking man stepped up to the bearded man you were with and claimed acquaintance with him as being one Netherfield Baxter?"

Jallanby started. It was plain that he remembered.

"I do," he acknowledged. "That sure enough happened. But the gentleman in question insisted there had been a mistake."

"I believe there was no mistake," said Scarterfield. "I'm of the opinion that man was Netherfield Baxter, and no other. Now, Mr. Jallanby, what do you know of these two?"

We had all been standing until then, but at this invitation to disclosure the ship-broker motioned us to sit down. He himself occupied the stool which the clerk had just vacated.

"This is a queer business, Mr. Scarterfield," he said. "Robbery? Murder? Pleasant, good-mannered, gentlemanly chaps I found 'em to be. Why, Lord bless me, I dined with 'em one night at their hotel!"

"Which hotel?" asked Scarterfield.

"The Station Hotel," replied Jallanby. "They were there for ten days or so. And in all that time, I never saw aught wrong with either of 'em. They seemed to be what they represented themselves to be. Certainly they'd plenty of money—for what they wanted here in Hull, anyway. But of course, that's neither here nor there."

"What names did you know them under?" inquired Scarterfield. "And where did they profess to come from?"

"Well, the man with the brownish beard called himself Mr.

Norman Belford," answered Jallanby. "I gathered he was from London. The other was a Frenchman—some lord or other, judging by his name, although I forget it in its entirety. Mr. Belford always called him *Vicomte*, which I took to be French for Viscount."

Scarterfield turned and regarded me, and I shot him a look that was no less significant. We were both thinking of the same thing—old Cazalette's find in the scrub near the beach at Ravensdene Court.

He turned back to the ship-broker. "Mr. Jallanby, what did these two want of you? What was their business in the city?"

"I can tell you that in a very few words," answered Jallanby. "They came in here one morning, told me they were staying at the Station Hotel, and said that they wanted to buy a small craft of some sort that a modest crew could run across the North Sea to the Norwegian fiords. They said they were both amateur yachtsmen, and, of course, I very soon found out that they knew what they were talking about. In fact, between you and me, I should have said that they were as experienced in sea-craft as any man could be."

"Aye," said Scarterfield, with a nod at me. "I dare say you would."

"Well, it so happened that I'd just the very thing they seemed to want," continued the ship-broker. "A vessel that had recently been handed over to me for disposal, lying in Victoria Dock, just at the back of here, beyond the old harbour. Just the sort of craft that they could sail themselves with a man or two. I can tell you exactly what she was, if you like."

Scarterfield nodded. "That might be useful to know. We may want to identify her."

"Well," said Jallanby, "she was a yawl about eighteen tons register; thirty tons yacht measurement; length forty-two feet; beam thirteen; draught seven and a half feet; square stern; coppered above the water-line; carried main, jib-headed mizen, and in addition had a sliding gunter gaff-topsail, and——"

"Enough!" interrupted Scarterfield with a smile. "That's all too technical for me to carry in my head! If we want details, I'll trouble you to write them down later. But I take it this vessel was all ready for going to sea?"

"Ready any day," asserted Jallanby. "Only just wanted tidying up and storing. As a matter of fact, she'd been in use quite recently, but she was a bit too solid for her late owner's tastes."

"Do I understand that this vessel could undertake a longish voyage?" asked Scarterfield. "For instance, could they have crossed the Atlantic in her?"

"Atlantic? Lord bless you, yes!" replied the ship-broker. "Or Pacific, for that matter. Go tens o' thousands o' miles in a craft of that soundness, as long as you've got provisions on board."

"So did they buy her?" asked Scarterfield.

"They did," replied Jallanby. "And paid the money there and then for her."

"Cheque?" inquired Scarterfield, laconically.

"No, sir—good Bank of England notes. They were all right as regards money—in my case, anyway. And you'll find the same as regards the tradesmen they dealt with. They fitted her out with provisions as soon as they'd got her."

"And then went off to Norway?" Scarterfield inquired.

"So I understand," assented Jallanby. "That's what they said at any rate. They were going first of all to Stavanger—then Bergen—then further north."

"Just the two of them?" asked Scarterfield.

"Why, no," replied Jallanby. "They were joined a day or two before they sailed by a friend of theirs—a Chinaman. A queer combination—Englishman, Frenchman, and Chinaman—but then again, stranger things happen at sea! This Chinaman was a real swell and Mr. Belford told me in private that he belonged to the Chinese Ambassador's suite in London."

Scarterfield raised an eyebrow. "Just so? A foreign dignitary. And where did he stop here?"

"Oh, he joined them at the hotel," answered Jallanby. "He'd

come there that night I dined with them. Quiet little chap—
quite the gentleman, you know."

"And his name?" asked Scarterfield.

The ship-broker held up a deprecating hand.

"Don't ask me!" he said. "I heard it, but I can't remember it
for the life of me. Still, you'd find it in the hotel register, no
doubt."

"How long is it since these chaps sailed for Bergen?" the
detective continued. "And what is the name of their smart little
vessel?"

"They sailed precisely three weeks ago next Monday,"
answered the ship-broker, "and the name of the vessel is the
Blanchflower."

"Good," said Scarterfield, well-satisfied with this rounded
information. "Now then for the moment, Mr. Jallanby, you'll
oblige me by keeping all this to yourself."

We left Mr. Jallanby then, promising to see him again, and
went away up the old High Street. I was wondering what the
detective made of all this, and I waited with some curiosity for
him to speak. When Scarterfield opened his mouth again, it was
to vent a good amount of scepticism.

"There's no way in a million years they've made for Norway.
Any more than that Chinese chap was attached to the Chinese
Legation. The whole thing's a bluff. By this time they'll have
altered the name of that yawl and gone in search of the buried
treasure."

"If the man who called himself Belford is really Baxter, he'll
know precisely where it is," I reasoned.

"Aye, just so, Mr. Middlebrook," assented Scarterfield.
"Although there's been time in all these years to shift that
stuff from one place to another. I haven't the slightest
doubt that Belford is Baxter, and that he and his associates
bought that vessel as the easiest way of getting the stuff
from wherever it's hidden. But where are we to look for
them?"

"If the man's Baxter, he must have gone north. The stuff is near Blyth – I feel certain of that."

"I believe you're right," the detective replied. "And I dare say a return to Blyth is the most advisable thing under the circumstances. After all, we know what to look out for—a twenty-ton yawl with an Englishman, a Frenchman, and a Chinaman aboard her!"

So that afternoon, after seeing the ship-broker again, and making certain arrangements with him in case he heard anything of the *Blanchflower*, we retraced our steps northward. But while Scarterfield turned off at Newcastle for Tynemouth and Blyth, I went forward alone for Alnwick and Ravensdene Court.

❄ 19 ❄

Being very late in the evening when I arrived at Alnwick, I remained there for the night, and it was not until noon of the next day that I once more reached Ravensdene Court. Lorrimore was there, having come over to lunch, and I hoped that he had brought some news from his Chinese servant, but the doctor had heard nothing of Wing since his departure. It would scarcely be Wing's method, he said, to communicate with him by letter. When he had anything to tell, he would either return forthwith or act of his own initiative upon the acquired information.

"And yourself, Middlebrook?" asked Mr. Raven. "What have you found out on your journeys?"

I told them the whole story as we sat at lunch. They were all deeply absorbed, but none more so than Mr. Cazalette, who gave me his complete and undivided attention. When he'd finally heard me out, he slipped away in silence, evidently very thoughtful, and disappeared into the library.

"So there it all is," I said in conclusion, "and if anybody can arrive at a definite and dependable theory, I am sure that Scarterfield will be glad to hear from them."

"It seems to me that Scarterfield is on the high road to a very respectable theory already," remarked Lorrimore. "But allow me to theorise a bit further, if I may. I haven't a doubt that these three murdered the Quicks and that they're now going to take up that swag which Baxter and the dishonest bank-manager safely planted somewhere. But I don't believe it's buried in any out-of-the-way place on the coast. I know where I should look for it, and where Scarterfield ought to search for it, if my hunch is correct."

"And where would that be?" I asked him.

"Well, the thing is to consider what those fellows were likely to do with the old monastic plate and jewels when they'd got them. They probably knew that the ancient chalices and reli-quaries would fetch big prices if sold privately to collectors— especially to American collectors, who, as everybody knows, are not at all squeamish about matters of provenance. I should say that Baxter, acting for his partner in crime, stored these things, and has waited for a favourable opportunity to resume posses-sion of them. I incline to the opinion that he stored them at Hartlepool, or at Newcastle, or at South-Shields—at any place whence they could easily be transferred by ship. He may, indeed, have stored them at Liverpool, for easy transit across the Atlantic. I don't believe in the theory that they're planted in some hole-and-corner along the coastline."

"Then how to account for Salter Quick's search for the graves of the Netherfields?" I queried him.

"Can't say," replied Lorrimore, with a shrug of his shoulders. "But Salter Quick may have got hold of the wrong tale, or half a tale, or mixed things up fundamentally. Anyway, that's my opinion—that this stolen property is not cached anywhere, but is somewhere within four respectable walls. If I were Scarter-field, I should communicate with stores and repositories asking for information about goods left with them some time ago and not reclaimed as yet."

"I agree," said Mr. Raven. "I find Lorrimore's theory more credible than the buried treasure notion."

"He makes a compelling case" I conceded, "but I can't help thinking Salter Quick's search for the graves of the Netherfields had some legitimate purpose."

Before Lorrimore could reply, Mr. Cazalette came back into the room, carrying a couple of fat quarto books under one arm, and a large folio under the other. As he came nearer the table with his big volumes, it became evident that he'd made some discovery and was anxious to tell us of it.

"Before you go any further," said he, laying down his burdens, "there are one or two things I should like to draw your attention to. Now about that monastic plate, Middlebrook, of which you've seen the inventories—you may not be aware of it, but there's a reference to that matter in Dryman's 'History of the Religious Foundations of Northumberland'."

Opening the dusty tome in question, Mr Cazalette read aloud from its tail end.

"*Abbey of Forestburne.*—It is well known that the altar vessels, plate, and jewels of this house, though considerable in number and value, were never handed over to the custodians of the King's Treasury House in London. They were duly inventoried by the receivers in these parts, and there are letters extant recording their dispatch, but they never reached their destination. It is commonly believed that these valuables were appropriated by high-placed persons of the neighbourhood who employed their underlings, marked and disguised, to waylay and despoil the messengers entrusted to carry them Southward. These foregoing remarks apply to the plate and jewels which appertained to the adjacent Priory of Mellerton, which were also of great worth."

"So," continued Mr. Cazalette, "there's no doubt in my mind that the plate of which Middlebrook saw the inventories is just what they describe it to be. And that it came into the hands of the late Lord Forestburne who deposited it in yon bank. And now," he went on, opening the biggest of his volumes, "here's the file of a local paper which your respected predecessor, Mr.

Raven, had the good sense to keep. In it, I've turned up the account of the inquest that was held at Blyth on yon dishonest bank manager. And there's a bit of evidence here that nobody seems to have drawn Scarterfield's attention to: 'The deceased gentleman,' it reads, 'was very fond of the sea, and frequently made excursions along our beautiful coast in a small yacht which he hired from Messrs. Capsticks, the well-known boat-builders of the town. It will be remembered that he had a particular liking for night-sailing, and would often sail his yacht out of harbour late of an evening in order, as he said, to enjoy the wonderful effects of moonlight on sea.'

"That, you'll bear in mind," concluded Mr. Cazalette, with a more than usually sardonic grin, "was penned by some fatuous reporter before they knew that the deceased gentleman had robbed the bank. And no doubt it was on those night excursions that he and this man Baxter carried away the stolen valuables, and safely hid them in some quiet spot along the coast. And there they'll all be found in good time, as sure as my name is what it is, Dr. Lorrimore. It was that spot that Salter Quick was after—only he wasn't exactly certain where it was, and had somehow got mixed up about the graves of the Netherfields. But man alive! yon plate of the old monks is buried under some head-stone hereabouts even as we speak!"

20

During the next few days, I heard nothing more from Scarterfield by post and could only presume that his investigations were ongoing. In the absence of news, myself and Miss Raven resumed our walks along the loneliest stretches of the coast. Before my journey to Blyth and Hull, she and I had already taken to going for long afternoon excursions together. Now we lengthened them again, going out after lunch and remaining away until we had only just time to return home by the dinner-hour. I think we had some vague idea that we might discover something of note, excited by Mr. Cazalette's feverish claims, although neither one of us spoke of this directly.

On Friday of that week, we travelled several miles from Ravensdene Court in a northerly direction. Seeking further novelty, we forwent the cliffs and headlands, following an inland track along the moors, which, for all their tortuous twists and turns, were never that far from the coastline. The last mile or two of this trail had been through absolute solitudes, save for a lonely farmstead or shepherd's cottage off in the distance. Nor that afternoon did we see any sail on the broad stretch of sea to our right, nor even the smoke-trail of a passing steamer on the horizon. Yet the place we now

approached seemed even more solitary. It was a sort of ravine—
a deep fissure in the line of the land—on the south side of
which lay a wood of ancient dwarf oak, so venerable and time-
worn in appearance that it looked like a survival of the Druid
age. There was not an opening to be seen in its thick undergrowth, nor any sign of path or track through it, but it was
with a mutual consent and understanding that we made our
way into its intense silence.

Beyond it, on the northern side, the further edge of this
ravine rose steeply, with masses of scarred limestone jutting out
of its escarpments. It seemed to me that at the foot of the wood,
and in the deepest part of this natural declension, there would
be a stream that ran downwards from the moor to the sea. I
think we had some idea of getting down to this, following its
course to the beach, and returning homeward by way of the
sands.

The wood into which we made our way was well-nigh
impregnable. It seemed to me that for age upon age the undergrowth had run riot—its strangely twisted boughs and tendrils
ever more matted and interwoven. It was only by turning in first
one, then another direction, that we made any kind of progress,
forcing our way between the tangle.

We exchanged laughing remarks about our having found the
forest primeval, and, before long, each was plentifully adorned
with scratches. All around us the silence was intense: there was
no singing of birds nor humming of insects. Altogether there was
an atmosphere of eeriness and gloom in that wood, and soon I
began—more for my companion's sake than my own—to long for
a glimpse of the sunlit sea beyond, or for the murmur of the
brook which I felt sure ran rippling coast-wards beneath this
almost impassable thicket.

All the while, Miss Raven bore this hardship with the
sporting spirit which was very much a part of her character.
Then, at the end of half-an-hour's struggle, she pushed her way
through a clump of wilding a little in advance of me.

"There's some building just in front of us!" she exclaimed. "It looks like an old ruin!"

Following her lead, and staring through the thickly-leaved branches, I saw a grey wall, venerable and time-stained. From here, I could make out the topmost stones, a sort of broken parapet with ivy clustering about it; and, beneath the green of the ivy, the cavernous gloom of a window place from which glass and tracery had long since gone.

"That's something to make for, anyway," I said. "Yet I don't remember anything of the sort marked on any local map."

We pushed forward again, and came out on a little clearing. Immediately in front of us stood the masonry of which we had caught glimpses: a low, squat, square tower, some forty feet high, ruinous for the most part, although the side now facing us was nearly perfect and still boasted a fine old doorway which I set down as of Norman architecture. North of this lay a mass of fallen masonry, a long line of weed-encumbered stone, which was evidently the ruin of one of its walls. Rank weed, bramble-bush, and beds of nettles all encumbered the place, adding to the sense of desolation. But a mere glance was sufficient to ascertain that we had chanced upon a once sacred spot.

"It must be the ruin of some ancient church or religious house," I surmised. "Look at the niche there above the arch of the door, and at the general run of the stone, it all points to a place of worship. It begs the question of why we've never heard of it. It appears to have fallen off the map."

"Utterly forgotten, I should think," said Miss Raven. "It must be a long time since there were people about here to come to it."

"Probably a village down on the coast, now swept away," I remarked. "But we must look this place out in the local books. Meanwhile, let's explore it."

Side by side, and stepping carefully, we began to look about the clearing, brooking a plenitude of bramble and gorse. In one place, a great clump of the latter had risen to such a height and thickness as to form an impenetrable barrier. Between this screen and the foot of the tower were great slabs of stone, over the edges of which coarse grass had grown, and whose surfaces were thickly encumbered with moss and lichen.

"Gravestones!" exclaimed Miss Raven.

No less thrilled, I got down on my knees before one of the slabs, less encumbered than the others, and began to tear away at the grass and weed. There was a rich, thick carpet of moss on it, and a fringe of grey, clinging lichen, but with the aid of a stout pocket-knife I forced it away and laid bare a considerable surface of the upper stone. With these growths removed, I could see lettering, worn and smoothed at its edges, but still to be made out with a little patience.

There may be a certain density in me, a slowness of intuition and perception, but it is a fact that at this time, and for some minutes later, I had not the faintest suspicion that we had accidentally lighted upon something connected with the mystery of Salter Quick. All I thought just then was that we had come across some old relic of antiquity—the church of some coastal hamlet or village which had long been left to rot. My only immediate interest was in deciphering the half-worn-out inscription on the stone by which I was kneeling. While my companion stood by me, watching with eager attention, I scraped out the earth and moss and lichen from the lettering. Fortunately, it had been deeply incised in the stone—which was of a hard and durable sort—and much of it remained legible. Presently I made out, at any rate, several words and figures:

Hic jacet dominus . . . Humfrey de Knaythville . . . quond' vicari huius . . . ecclie qui obéit . . . anno dei mccccxix

Beneath these lines were two or three others, presumably words of scripture, which had evidently become worn away before the moss spread its protecting carpet over the others. But we had learnt plenty for that and I regarded the result of my labours with proud satisfaction.

"There we are—'Here lies Master Humphrey de Knaythville,

sometime vicar of this church, who died in the year of our Lord one thousand four hundred and nineteen'."

"Splendid!" exclaimed Miss Raven, very much taken with our discovery. "I wonder if there are inscriptions on the other tombs?"

"No doubt," I assented, "and perhaps some other things of interest on this fallen masonry. This place is well worth careful examination, and I'm wondering how it is that I haven't come across any prior reference to it. Perhaps Mr. Cazalette can shed more light on the subject. We must make a full disclosure when we get back."

We began to look round again. This time I wandered around the base of the tower while Miss Raven explored the weed-choked ground towards the east end. Suddenly, from a short distance away, she gave a sharp, startled cry. Turning abruptly, I saw her standing by the great clump of overgrown gorse of which I have already spoken.

Rushing over, I asked concernedly what had prompted the shrill outburst.

Unconsciously, Miss Raven lowered her voice, glancing nervously at the thick undergrowth all around us, then pointed behind the gorse bush.

There behind the clump of green was what at first sight appeared to be a newly-opened grave, but was in reality a freshly-dug excavation. A heap of soil and stone, just flung out, lay all around it, and to one side rested a pick. Suddenly, I saw things for what they were. We had stumbled on the graveyard which Salter Quick had wished to find. De Knaythville and Netherfield were identical terms which had got mixed up in his uneducated mind, leading to the conflation of the two. Here the missing treasure was buried, and we had walked into this utterly deserted spot to interrupt its excavation.

Before I could say another word, I heard Miss Raven catch her breath, then move instinctively towards me. And in that same instant, I became aware of the presence of two men who had quietly stepped out from the shelter of the high undergrowth on the landward side of the clearing and stood silently watching us. They were attired in something of the fashion of seamen, in rough trousers and jerseys, but I saw at once that they were not common men. Indeed, I realized with a sickening feeling of apprehension that our wandering into that place had brought us face to face with marked danger. One of the two, a tallish, slender-built, good-looking man, I recognized as a stranger whom I had noticed at the coroner's inquest on Salter Quick and taken for some gentleman of the neighbourhood. The other, I felt sure, was Netherfield Baxter. He sported the golden-brown beard that Solomon Fish had mentioned, and had a half-hidden scar on his left cheek.

The four of us stood gazing at each other for what seemed to be a long and—to me—a painful minute. Then the man whom I took to be Baxter moved a little nearer to us.

"Well, sir," said he, lifting his cap as he glanced at Miss Raven. "Don't think me too abrupt, nor intentionally rude, if I ask you what you and this young lady are doing here?"

His voice was that of a man of education, even of refinement, but there was also something sharp and business-like about his manner, despite the seeming politeness. I saw at once that this was a man whose character was essentially matter-of-fact, and who would not allow himself to stick at trifles, for which reason I judged it best to be plain in my answer.

"We are here by sheer accident," I replied. "Exploring the wood for the mere fun of the thing. We chanced upon these ruins and have been examining them ever since."

"So you didn't come here with any set purpose?" he asked, looking us both over.

"Certainly not," said I. "We hadn't the faintest notion that such a place existed."

"But here it is, anyway," he said. "And so are you—in full possession of the knowledge. If I may ask, are you both tourists or do you live hereabouts?"

The other man made a remark under his breath in some foreign language, eyeing me all the while; after which, Baxter spoke again, still watching me.

"I think you, at any rate, are a resident," he said. "My friend has seen you before in these parts."

"I have seen him too," I said unthinkingly, "amongst the people at Salter Quick's inquest."

A meaningful glance passed between the two men, and Baxter's face grew notably sterner.

"Just so," he remarked. "That makes it all the more necessary that I seek further clarification regarding your identities."

"My name is Middlebrook, if you must know," I answered. "And I am not a resident of these parts—merely visiting here. As for this lady, she is Miss Raven, the niece of Mr. Francis Raven, of Ravensdene Court."

Baxter bowed politely to my companion as if I had just given him a formal introduction

"No harm shall come to you, Miss Raven," he said with apparent sincerity. "None whatsoever."

"Nor to Mr. Middlebrook, either, I should hope!" exclaimed Miss Raven, indignantly.

Baxter smiled in reply, showing a set of very white teeth.

"That depends," he said. "If Mr. Middlebrook behaves like a reasonable chap then we might still avoid any unpleasantness. With that aim in mind, may I ask if you're carrying any weapon?"

"A weapon!" I retorted scornfully. "Do you think I carry a revolver with me on an innocent country stroll?"

Baxter offered another smile, even more ambiguous than the last.

"One can never be too careful," he said. "There's no knowing with whom one might meet on one's travels."

"That may be so," I replied. "But we really must be leaving now. We shan't detain you any longer."

I motioned for Miss Raven to follow me, but Baxter laughed a little and shook his head.

"I'm not sure that we can allow that, just yet."

"Do you mean to tell me that you intend to interfere with our movements, just because you chance to find us here?" I demanded.

"Don't let us quarrel or get excited," he said, with a wave of his hand. "I have said that no harm shall come to you if you do as we ask."

Baxter stepped back to his companion and together they conferred in a low whisper.

"What does he mean?" murmured Miss Raven. "Do they intend to keep us here?"

"I don't know what they intend," I said. "But don't be afraid. I won't let anything untoward happen."

"I'm not afraid," she answered forthrightly. "Only I've a pretty good idea of who it is that we've just come across!"

"As have I," I replied. "But for the moment, I think we're both best served by complying with their wishes."

Baxter now turned back to us. "I'm sorry, but we can't let you go. The fact is, you've had the misfortune to light on a certain affair of ours about which we can't take any chances. We have a yacht nearby—you'll have to go with us on board and remain there for a day or two. No harm shall come to either of you—you have my word—if you only submit to this temporary inconvenience."

Now it was Baxter who motioned for us to leave, and led the way, while the other man followed behind myself and Miss Raven. There was nothing else to do except follow his bold directive. While I had given assurances that I was completely unarmed, I very much doubted the same was true of our new captors. So we went in silence, passing through the rest of the wood, along the side of the stream which I had expected to find, and to a small boat that lay hidden by the mouth of the creek. As they rowed us away in it, and rounded a spit of land, we saw the *Blanchflower* lying under a bluff beneath the cliffs. Ten minutes' of vigorous rowing brought us alongside the larger vessel, where I glanced up at her rail and caught a fleeting glimpse of another party. I barely had time to discern the man's features before they vanished, but they were clearly of Chinese descent.

21

In the few moments which elapsed between my catching
sight of that face peering at us from the rail, and our
setting foot on deck, I had time to arrive at a fairly conclu-
sive estimate of our situation. Without doubt we were in the
hands of Netherfield Baxter and his gang. Without doubt this
was the craft which they had bought from the Hull ship-broker.
And without doubt its presence on this lonely stretch of coastline was explained by the stolen treasure buried nearby.

I saw—or believed that I saw—the whole thing clearly. I was
not unduly concerned about myself—I fancied that I saw a
certain amount of honesty in Baxter's assurances—but I was
anxious about my companion, and about her uncle's anxiety.
Miss Raven was not the sort of young woman to be easily fright-
ened, but we were essentially defenceless, and amongst men who
were engaged in a dark and desperate adventure. Moreover, their
hands were probably far from clean in the matter of murder, and,
if the need arose, they would doubtless pay small regard to our
well-being or safety. Yet there was nothing else for it but to
accept the situation; at least for now.

The vessel was at anchor and lay in a sheltered cove, wherein,
I saw at a glance, she was lost to sight from the open sea. All was

quiet on her clean, freshly-scoured decks, and she looked, seen at close quarters, just what her possessors desired her to be taken for—a gentleman's pleasure yacht, the crew of which had nothing to do but keep her smart and bright. No one stepping aboard her would have suspected piracy or nefarious doings. As Miss Raven and I stood side by side, glancing about us with curiosity, a homely-looking grey cat came rubbing its shoulder against the woodwork. Meanwhile, a wisp of blue smoke escaped from the chimney of the cook's galley and we caught a whiff of a familiar sort—somebody, somewhere, was toasting bread or tea-cakes.

We stood idle, like prisoners awaiting orders, while our captors transferred from the boat to the yawl two biggish, iron-hooped chests, the wood of which was stained and discoloured with earth and clay. Being so heavy, the two men used tackle to get them aboard, setting them down close by where we stood. Having done so, Baxter came over to us, rubbing from his fingers the soil which had gathered on them. He smiled politely, with something of the air of a host who wants to apologise for the only accommodation he can offer.

"Now, Miss Raven," he said, with an air of benevolent indulgence, "as we shall be obliged to inflict our hospitality upon you for a day or two, let me show you what we can give you in the way of quarters. We can't offer you the services of a maid, but there is a good cabin, well fitted, in which you'll be comfortable and might regard as your own domain for the duration of your stay."

He led us down a short gangway, and across a small saloon, evidently used as a common-room by himself and his companion. Beyond it, he threw open the door of a neat though very small cabin.

"Never been used," he said with another smile. "Fitted up by the previous owner of this craft, and all in tip-top order, as you can see. Consider it as your own, Miss Raven. One of my men shall see that you've whatever you need in the way of towels and hot water. You'll find him as handy as a French maid. Give him any orders or instructions you like. Then come on deck again, if you please, and we shall all have some tea."

He beckoned me to follow him as Miss Raven walked into her quarters, and gave me a reassuring look as we crossed the outer cabin.

"She'll be perfectly safe and secluded in there," he said. "You can mount guard here if you like, Mr. Middlebrook. In fact, this is the only place I can offer you for quarters. I dare say you can manage to make a night's rest on one of these lounges, with the help of some rugs and cushions."

"I'm all right," said I. "Don't trouble about me. My only concern is with Miss Raven."

"I'll take good care that Miss Raven is safe in everything," he answered. "As safe as if she were in her uncle's house. So don't bother your head on that score."

"As regards her uncle," I said, "I want to speak to you about him. Mr. Raven will be in a state of great anxiety about his niece. She is the only relative he has, I believe, and he will be extremely anxious if she does not return this evening."

"I've thought of that," he said airily. "As a matter of fact, my friend whom you met up there at the ruins is going ashore again in a few minutes. He will go straight to the nearest telegraph office, which is a mile or two inland, and there he will send a wire to Mr. Raven, addressed from you, which should arrive by, say, seven o'clock."

"That's all very well," I answered, "but how do you expect me to word it?"

"Say that you and Miss Raven find you cannot get home tonight, having briefly lost your way, and have taken refuge at a hostelry."

"That might do at a pinch for one night, if we are free to return tomorrow. I cannot see it passing muster any longer than that."

"Tomorrow night is a possibility," Baxter answered. "I will do my best. I hope to be through with my business by tomorrow afternoon."

At that moment the other man appeared on deck again, having changed his clothes, presenting himself now in a smart tweed suit, Homburg hat, polished shoes, and with an elegant walking cane. While Baxter regarded him, showing signs of satisfaction, I wrote out a message which I hoped would allay Mr. Raven's anxieties for the night.

After Baxter had read it, he nodded in approbation.

"It should be delivered to Ravensdene Court by eight," he said. "So there's no need to worry further—you can tell Miss Raven that. And when all's said and done, Mr. Middlebrook, it wasn't my fault that you broke in upon very private doings up there in the old churchyard—nor, I suppose, yours either. Please make the best of it—it's only a temporary detention."

I watched him closely as he talked, and suddenly made up my mind to speak out, despite the dangers. For some reason, I had an intuitive feeling that it constituted a worthwhile risk.

"I believe," I said, brusquely enough, "that I am speaking to Mr. Netherfield Baxter?"

He returned me a sharp glance which was half-smiling and less astonished than I'd reckoned on. "Aye," he answered. "I thought you might be thinking that. Well, and suppose I admit it, Mr. Middlebrook? What do you presume to know of me?"

The man's air of proud complacency encouraged me to answer his question at some length.

"That you formerly lived at Blyth, and had some association with a certain temporary bank-manager there, about whose death—and the disappearance of some valuable property—there was a good deal of concern manifested. That you were never heard of again until recently, when a Blyth man recognized you in Hull, where you bought a yawl—this yawl, I believe—and said you were going to Norway. Should I go on, sir? Would you have me be yet more explicit?"

"Why not?" said he with a laugh. "Forewarned is forearmed. You're giving me valuable information."

"Very well, Mr. Baxter," I continued, determined to show him my cards. "There's a certain detective, one Scarterfield, who is very anxious to make your acquaintance. For if you want the plain truth, he believes you, or some of your accomplices, to have had a hand in the murders of Noah and Salter Quick. And he's on your track, mark my words—you can rest assured of that!"

I was watching him still more closely as I spoke the last sentence or two, but Baxter remained as calm and cool as ever; and I was somewhat taken aback by the collected fashion in which he replied to my provocation at length.

"Scarterfield—of whose doings I've heard a bit—has got hold of the wrong end of the stick there, Mr. Middlebrook," he said quietly. "I had no hand in murdering either Noah Quick or his brother Salter; nor had my friend—the man who's just gone off with your telegram. I don't know whose to blame exactly, but there have always been those ready to carry out the deed if they got the chance, and I wasn't the least surprised to hear of the brothers' passing. The only wonder is that they escaped murder as long as they did! But beyond the fact that they were murdered, I know nothing—nor does anybody on board this craft, I can assure you. You may call us pirates if you like, buccaneers, adventurers, anything of the sort—but not assassins."

I believed him. And made haste to say so—out of sheer relief that Miss Raven was not amongst men whose hands were stained with blood.

"Thank you," he said, as coolly as ever. "I'm obliged to you. I've been anxious enough to know who did murder those two men."

"You knew them—the Quicks?" I suggested.

Baxter nodded readily. "They were a couple of rank bad 'uns and no mistaking! I have never professed sanctity, Mr. Middlebrook, but Noah and Salter Quick were of a different brand altogether. But look, here comes Miss Raven—let's settle down to our tea."

While he went forward to give his orders, I contrived to inform Miss Raven of the gist of our conversation, and to assert my own private belief in Baxter's innocence. I saw that she was already prejudiced in his favour.

"I'm glad to hear that," she said. "But in that case, this mystery's all the deeper. What is it, I wonder, he can tell?"

Baxter came back presently, followed by a small framed Chinaman, who deftly set up a table on deck, drew chairs round it, and a few minutes later spread out a dainty afternoon tea in the centre of which lay a resplendent plum cake.

Despite our sorry plight—prisoners for all intents and purposes—there was an unmistakable air of civility to our small gathering. All three of us sat round the table, munching toast, nibbling cakes and dainties, and sipping fragrant tea, as if we were in a lady's drawing-room. At the outset, we talked about anything but the prime fact of our imprisonment. Baxter, indeed, might have been our very polite and attentive host and we his willing guests.

As for Miss Raven, she accepted the whole thing with hearty good humour and poured out the tea as if she had been familiar with our new quarters for many a long day. Moreover, she adopted a friendly attitude towards our captor which helped to smooth over any present difficulties.

"You seem to be very well accommodated in the matter of servants, Mr. Baxter," she observed. "That Chinaman, as you said, is as good as a French maid, and you certainly have a an excellent pastry-cook."

Baxter glanced lazily in the direction of the galley. "Another gentleman from the East, as it happens." Then he turned and looked at me. "Mr. Middlebrook is aware—as you may or may not know—that I bought this yawl from a ship-broker in Hull for a special purpose."

"That might be," I answered good-humouredly. "But I must still profess ignorance of what that special purpose is."

"A run across the Atlantic, if you want to know," he answered carelessly. "Of course, when I'd got her, I wanted a small crew. Now, I've had great experience of Chinamen—hardest workers on earth in my opinion—so I sailed her down to the Thames, went up to London Docks, and took in some chaps at Limehouse. Two men and one cook, which is why, although I can't promise you a real and proper dinner tonight, you can look forward to a very satisfactory substitute."

"And you're going across the Atlantic with a crew of three?" I asked.

"As a matter of fact," he answered candidly, "there are six of us in total. The three Chinese, myself, my friend who was with me this afternoon, and another friend who will return with him —also a Chinaman—although he's one of rank and position."

"In other words, the Chinese gentleman who was with you and your French friend in Hull?" I suggested.

"Just so—since we're to be frank," he answered. Then, with a laugh, he glanced at Miss Raven. "Mr. Middlebrook considers me the most candid desperado he ever met!"

"Your candour is certainly interesting," replied Miss Raven. "Especially if you really are a desperado. Perhaps you'll give us more of it?"

"I'll tell you a bit later on," he said. "About that Quick business. But you'll excuse me for the moment."

Setting down his tea cup, Baxter got up and moved away towards the galley, into which he disappeared presently.

As soon as we were alone, Miss Raven turned sharply on me.

"Did you eat a slice of that plum cake?" she whispered.

"I know what you're thinking," I answered. "It reminds you of the cake that Wing served at Lorrimore's house."

"Reminds!" she exclaimed. "There's no reminding about it! Do you know what I think? Wing is aboard this yacht right now!"

22

There was so much of real importance in Miss Raven's confident suggestion that her words immediately plunged me into a thoughtful silence. Rising from my chair, I walked across to the landward side of the yawl, and stood there, reflecting. But it needed little reflection to convince me that what my fellow prisoner had just suggested was well within the bounds of possibility. I recalled all that we knew of the recent movements of Dr. Lorrimore's Chinese servant. Wing had gone to London on the pretext of finding out something about his problematical countryman, Lo Chuh Fen. Since his departure, Lorrimore had had no tidings of him and his doings—in Lorrimore's opinion, he might be still in London, or he might have gone to Liverpool, to Cardiff, or any other port where his compatriots were to be found in England. So it was far from impossible that Wing, having been in Limehouse or Poplar, and in touch with Chinese sailors there, should have taken service with Baxter and his accomplice, and, at that very moment, been within a few yards of Miss Raven and myself. But why? If he was there in that yawl, then in what real capacity? Ostensibly, as cook, no doubt—but there had to be much more to it than that.

Was this his way of finding out what all of us wanted to

know? And if it came to it—such occasion as I dared not contemplate—could Miss Raven and myself count on Wing as a friend, or should we find him an adherent of this curious gang, who, if the truth was to be faced, held not only our liberty, but our lives at its disposal? For we were in a tight place—of that there was no doubt. Up to that moment, I was not unimpressed by Netherfield Baxter, and, whether against my better judgment or not, I was inclined to believe him innocent of complicity in the murders of Noah and Salter Quick. But I could see that he was a strange mortal: candid and frank on account of his vanity, and given to talking a good deal about himself and his doings to the point of megalomania.

He might treat us well so long as things went well with him, but supposing a situation were to arise in which our presence, nay, our very existence, became a danger to him and his long-standing ambitions? He had a laughing lip and a twinkle of sardonic humour in his eye, but I fancied that the lip could settle into ruthless resolve if need be, and the eye become more stony than would be pleasant. Moreover, we were at his mercy. The mercy of a man whose accomplices might be of a worse kind than himself, willing to slit a throat at the faintest sign from their master.

As I stood there, staring gloomily at the shore—so near and yet so impossible of access—I reviewed a point which was of more importance to me than may be imagined. I have already said that the yawl lay at anchor in a sheltered cove, but the position of that cove was noteworthy. It was entered by way of an extremely narrow inlet, across the mouth of which stretched a bar—I could see this by watching the breakers rolling over it. It was therefore plain that even a small vessel could only get in or out of the cove at high water. But once across the bar, and within the narrow entry, any vessel would find itself in a natural harbour of great advantage. The cove ran inland for a good mile, and was quite another mile in width. Its waters were deep, rising some fifteen to twenty feet over a clear, sandy bottom, and it was sheltered by high cliffs whose headlands were, in turn, covered by thick woodland.

That the cove was known to the folk of that neighbourhood, it was impossible to doubt, but I felt sure that any strange craft passing along the sea in front would never suspect its existence, so carefully had Nature concealed the entrance. And there were no signs within the cove itself that any of the shore folk ever used it. Furthermore, I knew myself that an equal desolation lay all over the land immediately behind the cove and its sheltering woods. For some miles, north and south, there was nothing save an isolated farmstead set in deep ravines at wide distances. The only link with busier things lay in the railway—some two-and-a-half miles inland, as far as I could recollect from the map which lay in my pocket, but which I did not dare to pull out. All things considered, Miss Raven and I were as securely trapped, and as much at our captor's mercy, as if we had been immured in a twentieth-century Bastille.

Presently, I went back to the tea table and dropped into my chair again. Baxter was still away from us, as far as I could tell.

Miss Raven, despite her admirable bravura, had a few doubts of her own that began to surface.

"What do you suppose is going to happen to us?" she asked, glancing over her shoulder at the open door of the galley.

"I think they'll detain us until they're ready to depart, and then they'll release us," I answered. "At which point, Baxter will probably ask that we say nothing of this to anyone.."

"He could have done that without bringing us here," she remarked.

"Ah, but he wanted to make sure," I told her. "However, I don't think he means to harm us. Under other conditions, I shouldn't have objected to meeting him. He's certainly an interesting character."

"Do you think he really is a pirate?" Miss Raven asked.

"In truth, I would not put it past him. Either way, I'm sure we shall hear more on the subject—and subjects pertaining to it —before we get our freedom back."

In this last regard, I was correct. Throughout the late afternoon, and into the evening, Baxter behaved like a man who for a long time had had small opportunity of conversation. He was a good talker, too, and knew much of books and politics, and of men, and could make shrewd remarks, tinged with a little cynicism that was more good-humoured than bitter.

The time passed rapidly in this fashion. Supper arrived, and the meal was as good and substantial as any dinner. It was served by the soft-footed Chinaman, who, other than Baxter, was the only living soul we had seen since the Frenchman had left the boat. Sitting in the small, saloon-like cabin, Baxter kept up his ready flow of talk while observing his hostly duties. Until then, the topics had been of a general nature, such as one might have heard dealt with at any gentleman's table. But when supper was over, and the Chinaman had left us alone, he smiled at me and Miss Raven in turn, a curious gleam in his eye.

"You think me an odd fellow, I'm sure" he said. "And yet I've barely touched on my idiosyncrasies . . ."

I made no reply beyond an acquiescent nod, but Miss Raven —who all through this adventure had shown a coolness and resourcefulness which I can never praise sufficiently—looked steadily at him.

"I think you must have seen and known some strange things," she responded.

"Aye—and done some!" he answered with a raucous laugh, before turning to glance at me. "Mr. Middlebrook knows a bit about me and my affairs," he said. "Sufficient, at least, to whet his curiosity."

"I confess I should like to know more," I replied. "I agree with Miss Raven—you must have seen a good deal that exceeds a man's regular experience."

There was some fine old claret on the table between us. Now Baxter pushed the bottle over, motioning me to refill my glass.

For a moment he sat, silently reflecting—a cigar in the corner of his lips, and his hands in the armholes of his waistcoat.

"What's really puzzling you, no doubt, is the true basis of this Quick affair," he said suddenly.

"So allow me to offer you what I can in the way of illumination. For at one time I knew the Quicks as well as any man living. Not a nice story from a moral point of view, but no less instructive for that."

We made no answer, so he refilled his glass, and took a mouthful of its contents, before continuing with his narrative.

"You're both aware of my youthful career at Blyth?" he said. "You are anyway, Middlebrook, from what you told me this afternoon, and I gather that you've put Miss Raven in possession of the facts already. Well, I'll start out from there—when I made the acquaintance of that bank manager chappie. Mind, I'd about come to the end of my tether at that time as regards money, largely through reckless ignorance and youthful folly. Although I was robbed by more than one worthy man of my native town—legally, of course, god bless 'em! And that's why I deemed it only fair and proper that I get my own back.

"Now that bank manager chap was one of those fellows who are born with predatory instincts. My impression of him, from what I recollect, is that he was a born thief. Anyway, he and I, getting pretty thick with each other, found out that we were actuated by similar ambitions. I from sheer necessity, he from ingrained temperament. And to cut matters short, we determined to help ourselves to certain things of value stored in that bank, and to clear out to far-off regions on the proceeds. To that end, we discovered that two chests deposited in the bank's vaults by old Lord Forestburne contained invaluable monastic spoil, stolen by the good man's ancestors four centuries before.

"The plan was to take it over to the United States, where we knew we could realize immense sums on it from unscrupulous collectors. So having carefully removed the lot, and brought them along the coast to this very cove, we interred them in those ruins where we three foregathered this afternoon."

"And whence, I take it, you have just removed them to the deck above our heads?" I suggested.

"Right, Middlebrook! Quite right you are!" he acknowledged jovially. "A grand collection it is too—chalices, patens, reliquaries, all manner of splendid mediaeval craftsmanship, and certain other more modern things with them. All destined for the other side of the Atlantic, where the market's sure and ready—"

"You think you'll get them there?" I asked.

"I certainly do," he answered readily. "I'm a dab hand at carrying out a plan to perfection. Yes, sir, they'll be there in good time—and they'd have been there a lot sooner if it wasn't for an unforeseeable accident. How could I have known the bank-manager would have the ill-luck to break his neck? Now that put me in a quandary as I knew the whole affair would soon be discovered, and that I'd need to exercise great care in covering up all trace of my own share in it. So, knowing the stuff was safely planted and unlikely to be disturbed, I cleared out and determined to wait upon a fitting opportunity."

Throwing away the stump of his cigar, Baxter deliberately lighted another, and leaned across the table towards me in a more confidential manner.

"After I cleared out of Blyth—with a certain amount of money in my pocket—I knocked about the world a good deal, doing one thing and another. I've been in every continent and in more seaports than I can possibly remember. I've taken a share in all sorts of queer transactions—smuggling among them. I've been rolling in money in January and shivering in rags in June, and rarely known a happy median. I could tell you enough to fill a dozen fat volumes, but we'll cut all that out and get on to a certain time, some years ago, when I and the Frenchman you saw with me this afternoon found ourselves in Hong Kong. It was there, thanks to a cruel twist of fate, we crossed paths with Noah and Salter Quick."

"Was that the first time you'd met them?" I interjected. Now that Baxter was intent on telling me his story, I, on my part, was bent on getting out of him all that I could.

"Never seen nor heard of them before," he answered. "We met in a certain den of iniquity in Hong Kong, much frequented by Englishmen and Americans, where we soon enough became fast friends. Like ourselves, they were adventurers, would-be pirates, minded to pursue any dubious venture. We found out, too, that they had money behind them, and could finance any desperate affair that was likely to pay handsomely.

"My friend and I, at that time, were also in funds—we had just had a very paying adventure in the Malay Archipelago. That's why we'd journeyed on to Hong Kong on the look-out for another opportunity. Once we'd got in with the Quicks, that was not long in coming, for the brothers were as sharp as their name and knew exactly the sort of men they wanted. Before long, they took us into their confidence and told us what they were after and what they wanted us to do. The idea was to get hold of a ship and use it for certain nefarious trading purposes in the China seas. Needless to say, we were ready enough to go in with them, especially as their plans were well advanced.

"There was at that time lying at Hong Kong a sort of tramp steamer, the *Elizabeth Robinson*, the skipper of which wanted a crew for a trip to Chemulpo. Salter Quick got himself into the good graces of this skipper, and offered to man his ship for him, packing here as far as he could with those he trusted. That included his brother Noah, myself, my French friend, and a certain Chinese cook of his longstanding acquaintance."

"Am I right in supposing the name of the Chinese cook to have been Lo Chuh Fen?" I asked.

"Quite right—Lo Chuh Fen was the man," answered Baxter, not blinking an eye at my knowledge. "A handy man for anything, you have to admit, for he's the very same chap who served us supper this evening. Having come across him again in Limehouse recently, I took him into my service once more. Very well—now you understand that there were five of us in for the Quick's plan, I should add that Salter planned to get round the rest of the crew by way of promises and outright bribery. That done, we were going to put the skipper, his mates, and such of the men as wouldn't fall in with us, in a boat with provisions and let them find their way wherever they liked while we went off with the steamer. Such at least was the surface plan—although my own belief is that the Quicks would have been ready to make skipper and men walk the plank if it came to that. Both Noah and Salter, for all their respectable appearance, were born out of their time and would have made admirable lieutenants to Paul Jones or any other eighteenth-century pirate! But in this particular instance, their schemes came to nothing. The skipper of the *Elizabeth Robinson* was an American, and cuter than we'd fancied. So it was one morning, having got wind of our plans, he turned the tables on us, sure enough. Our band of would-be mutineers was bundled into a boat at gunpoint and pointed in the direction of the nearest small island. Instead of taking over the steamer, we found ourselves marooned in effect . . ."

23

The word "marooned" was spoken with a special emphasis which showed that it awoke no very pleasant memories in Netherfield Baxter.

Miss Raven looked at him questioningly.

"Marooned?" she said. "What is that, exactly?"

Baxter gave her an indulgent smile.

"I dare say Mr. Middlebrook can give you the exact etymological meaning of the word better than I can, Miss Raven," he answered. "But I can tell you what the thing means in actual practice. To put men ashore on a desert island, leaving them to fend for themselves as best they're able. Oftentimes, this leads to slow starvation—at best it means living on what you can pick up by your own ingenuity."

"You had a stiff time of it?" I suggested.

Baxter winced at the abiding memory. "Worse than you'd believe," he answered. "That old Yankee skipper was a vindictive chap with plenty of method in him. He'd purposely gone off the beaten track to land us on that island, and he played his game so cleverly that not even the Quicks—who were as subtle as snakes —knew anything of his intentions until we were all marched over the side at the point of ugly-looking revolvers. If it hadn't been for that unassuming Chinaman whom you've just seen we would have starved, for the island was little more than a reef of rock, rising to a sort of peak in its centre, and with nothing edible on it in the way of flesh or fruit. But Chuh was a Godsend. He was clever at fishing, showed us an edible seaweed out of which he made good eating, and also discovered a spring of water. He kept us all alive. Of that, there can be no doubting. All of which made the conduct of those two Quicks all the more devilish . . ."

"What did they do?" I asked.

"All in due course," Baxter replied, holding a hand up to stay my questioning. "As it was, we were on that island several weeks, and from the time we were flung unceremoniously upon its miserable shores, we hadn't seen a sail nor a wisp of smoke from a steamer. And it may be that this, and our other privations, made us still more birds of a feather. Men thrown together in that way will talk—nay, they must talk!—about their past doings and so on. We used to tell tales of our doubtful pasts as we huddled together under the rocks at nights, and some nice, lurid stores there were, I can assure you! The Quicks had seen about as much of the doubtful and seamy side of seafaring life as men could, although all of us could contribute something. They had money safely stowed away in banks here and there, and used to curse their fate when they thought of it. And it was that, I think, that led me to tell of my adventure with the naughty bank manager at Blyth, and of the chests of old monastic treasure which I'd planted up here on the Northumbrian coast."

"Ah!" I exclaimed. "So you told the Quicks about that?"

"I did," he replied sombrely. "But when I told them all about the Blyth affair, I didn't believe we should ever get away from that cursed island. That said, I explained things in a fashion which evidently led to considerable puzzlement on their part. I told them that I buried the chests in a churchyard on this coast, close to the graves of my ancestors, describing the lie of the ruins pretty accurately. Now where the Quicks must have got puzzled was over my use of the word 'ancestors'. What I meant —but never said—was that I had planted the stuff near the graves of my maternal ancestors, the old De Knaythevilles, who were once great folk in these parts, and of whose name my own is, of course, a corruption. But Salter Quick, to be sure, thought the graves would bear the name Netherfield, and when he came along this coast, it was that name he was hunting for."

"So he was after that treasure?" I said.

"Of course he was!" replied Baxter. "The only wonder to me is that he and Noah hadn't been after it before. But they were men who had a good many irons in the fire—some of them far too hot, as it turned out!—and I suppose they left this little affair until an opportune moment. Without a doubt, not so long after I'd told them the story, Salter Quick scratched inside the lid of his tobacco box a rough diagram of the place I'd mentioned, with the latitude and longitude approximately indicated. That's the box there's been so much fuss about and I'll tell you more about it in due process.

"But now about that island, and how they and the rest of us got off it. I told you that the centre rose to a high peak, separating one coast from the other. One day, after several weary weeks, I, my French friend, and the Chinaman crossed its shoulder, prospecting out of sheer desperation. We spent the next night on the other side of the island, and it was not until late on the following afternoon that we returned to our crude base camp. When we got back, Noah and Salter Quick were gone and the Chinaman's sharp eyes soon accounted for their disappearance. A distant sail could just be seen vanishing over the horizon. Some Chinese fishing boat had made that island in our absence, and these two skunks had gone away in her and left us to fend for ourselves. That's the sort the Quicks were and that's how much stock they placed in friendship! Do you wonder then, either one of you, that they eventually got what was coming?"

We made no answer to that, beyond a shake of our heads, until Miss Raven spoke up.

"But you got away in the end?" she reasoned.

"That we did—some time later, when we were just about done for," assented Baxter. "And in the same way—a Chinese fishing boat that came within reach. It landed us on the Kiang-Su coast and we still had a pretty bad time of it before making our way back to Shanghai. From that port we worked our passage to Hong Kong. I had an idea that we might strike the Quicks there, or get news of them, but we heard nothing of those two villains. However, we did hear that the *Elizabeth Robinson* had gone down with all hands, and we were supposed, of course, to have gone down with her. Both I and my friend had money in Hong Kong, and we took it up and went off to Singapore without disabusing anybody of the notion. As for our Chinaman, Chuh said farewell to us and we never set eyes on him again until very recently, when I ran across him in a Chinese eating-house in Poplar."

"From that meeting, I suppose, the more recent chapters of your story begin?" I suggested. "Or do they begin somewhat earlier?"

"A bit earlier," he said. "My friend and I came back to England a little before that with money in our pockets, and in the company of a Chinese gentleman. We decided to go in for a little profitable work of another sort, and to start out by lifting my concealed belongings up here. So we bought this craft in Hull, then ran her down to the Thames before coming across Lo Chuh Fen and hiring two more of his compatriots."

Pausing to fill his glass again, Baxter looked up and regarded us evenly.

"You know that some men in my position would have thought nothing about putting bullets through both of you when we met this afternoon. But I'm not that sort—I treat you as what you are, a gentlewoman and a gentleman, and no harm shall come to either of you. Therefore, I feel certain that all I've said will be treated as it ought to be. I dare say you think I'm an awful scoundrel, yet I haven't the slightest compunction about appropriating the stuff in those chests. One of the Forestburnes stole it from the monks—why shouldn't I steal it from his successor? It's as much mine as his—perhaps more so, for one of my ancestors, a certain Geoffrey de Knaytheville, was at one time Lord Abbot of the very house that the Forestburnes stole that stuff from. I've a good prior claim, if you ask me."

"I should imagine," I answered guardedly, "that it would be difficult for anybody to substantiate a claim to ecclesiastical property which disappeared in the sixteenth century. What is certain, however, is that you've got it. Now if you'll take my advice, Baxter, you'll hand it over to the authorities."

He looked at me in blank astonishment for a moment; then laughed at the top of his voice as he pushed the claret nearer. "You're a born humorist, friend Middlebrook! Hand it over to the authorities? Why, that would merit a full-page cartoon in the next number of *Punch!*"

"Needless to say, it is not the plate alone that concerns the authorities," I told him.

"You're talking of the Quicks' murder? Well, that's a very easy point to settle, if it should ever come to it," he answered. "And I'll settle it for your own edification, right away. Noah and Salter Quick were done to death—one in Saltash, the other near Alnwick—about the same hour of the same evening. Now my friend and I, so far from being anywhere near either Saltash or Alnwick, spent that particular night together at the North Eastern Railway Hotel at York. I went there that afternoon from London, and he joined me from Berwick. We met at the hotel about six o'clock, dined within it, played billiards, and then were away to bed. I dare say the hotel folks will remember us well, and our particulars are registered in their books on the date in question. We had no hand whatever in the murders of Noah and

Salter Quick, and I give you my word of honour—for what it's worth—that I haven't the slightest notion who did!"

Miss Raven made an involuntary murmur of approval, and I was so much convinced of the man's good faith that I stretched out my hand to him.

"Mr. Baxter!" said I, "I'm heartily glad to have that assurance from you! And whether I'm a humorist or not, I'll beg you once more to take my advice and give up that loot to the authorities. You can make a plausible excuse, throw all the blame on that bank manager fellow, and then devote your undoubtedly great and able talents to legitimate ventures."

"That would be as dull as ditch-water, Middlebrook" he retorted with a grin. "Although I won't say you're not tempting me! As for those Quicks—I'll tell you in what fashion there is a connection between their murder and ourselves, and one that would need some explanation. Bear in mind that I've kept myself apprised of those crimes through the newspapers, and also by collecting a certain amount of local gossip. Now you've a certain somewhat fussy and garrulous old gentleman at Ravensdene Court . . ."

"Mr. Cazalette!" exclaimed Miss Raven.

"Mr. Cazalette is the name," said Baxter, "and I have heard a great deal of him through the sources I've just referred to. Now this Mr. Cazalette, going to or coming from a place where he bathed every morning, which place happened to be near the spot where Salter Quick was murdered, found a blood-stained hand-kerchief as I understand it?"

"He did," said I. "And a lot of mystery attaches to it."

"That handkerchief belongs to my French friend," said Baxter. "I told you that he joined me at York from Berwick. As a matter of fact, for some little time just before the Salter Quick affair, he was down on this coast, posing as a tourist, while ascertaining if things were as I'd left them at the ruins and what would be our best method of transporting the chests away. For a week or so, he lodged at an inn near Ravensdene Court and used to go down to the shore for a swim himself on certain mornings. On one of these, he cut his foot on the pebbles and staunched the blood with his handkerchief, which he carelessly threw away, leading to Mr. Cazalette's discovery. Then there's this business of the tobacco box to contend with . . ."

"A much more important point," said I.

"Just so," agreed Baxter. "Now, my friend and I first heard of the murder while we were at York. In the newspapers, there was an account of a conversation which took place in Mr. Raven's coach-house, or some other outbuilding, whither the dead man's body had been carried. It was conducted by old Mr. Cazalette and a police inspector, regarding a certain metal tobacco box found on Salter Quick's body. Now I give you my word this was the first intimation we'd had that the Quicks were back in England. Until then we hadn't the slightest idea that they were here, but we knew right enough what those mysterious scratches on the tobacco box lid signified—Salter had made a rude plan of the place and was in Northumberland to search for it.

"Later on, we read your evidence at the opening of the inquest, and heard what you had to tell about his quest for the Netherfield graves. And so—just to satisfy ourselves—we determined to get hold of that tobacco box to negate the risk of somebody discovering our buried valuables. That's why my friend came down again in his tourist capacity, put up at the same quarters, attended the adjourned inquest as a casual spectator, and abstracted the tobacco box under the very noses of the police! It's in that locker now," continued Baxter, with a laugh, pointing to a corner of the cabin, "and with it are the handkerchief and Mr. Cazalette's pocket-book——"

"Oh! your friend got that, too, did he!" I answered.

Baxter gave a pleased shrug. "Naturally, we weren't going to take any chances."

I remained silent awhile, reflecting.

"It's a very fortunate thing for both of you that you could, if necessary, prove your presence at York on the night of the murder," I remarked at last. "Your recent conduct might otherwise wear a very suspicious look. As it is, I'm afraid the police would probably say that even if you and your French friend didn't murder Salter Quick and his brother, you were probably accessory to both murders. That's how it strikes me, anyway."

"I think you're right," he said calmly. "Probably they would. But we were not accessory, either before or since. We haven't the ghost of a notion as to the identity of the Quicks' murderers. But since we're discussing that, I'll tell you something that seems to have completely escaped the notice of the police, the detectives, and yourself. You remember that in both cases the clothing of the murdered men had been literally ripped to pieces?"

I nodded. "It had in Salter's case—I can vouch for that."

"And so, they said, it had in Noah's," replied Baxter. "And the presumption, of course, was that the murderers were searching for something."

"Of course," I said. "What other presumption could there be?"

Baxter gave us both a keen, knowing look, bent across the table, and tapped my arm as if to arrest my closer attention.

"How do you know that the murderers didn't find what they were seeking for?" he asked in a low, forceful voice.

I stared at him; so, too, did Miss Raven, prompting another burst of laughter.

"That doesn't seem to have struck anybody," he said.

"I'd never thought of it," I admitted.

"Exactly. Nor, according to the papers—and my private information—had anybody else. Yet it would have been the very first thought that occurred to me had I chanced on either crime scene."

"Perhaps with your knowledge of the Quicks' queer doings," I replied, "you have some knowledge of what they might be likely to carry about them?"

He laughed at that, and again leaned nearer to us.

"Aye, well!" he replied. "As I've told you so much, I'll tell you something more in addition. I do know of something that the two men had on them when they were on that miserable island and that they carried away with them when they escaped from it. Noah and Salter Quick were in possession of two magnificent rubies, the like of which I'd never seen before!"

⚜ 24 ⚜

I could not repress an involuntary start on hearing this remarkable declaration. It seemed to open, as widely as suddenly, an entirely new field of vision.

Seeing my look of surprise, Baxter laughed significantly.

"That strikes you forcibly, Middlebrook—does it not?"

"Very forcibly, indeed," said I. "If what you say is true, then there's a reason for their murders that none of us knew of. But is it probable that the Quicks would still be in possession of jewels that you saw some years ago?"

"Not so many years ago, when all's said and done," he answered. "And you couldn't dispose of things like those very readily. You can take it from me, knowing what I did of them, that neither Noah nor Salter Quick would sell anything unless at its full value. They weren't hard up for money and could afford to wait until they found a buyer who'd meet their asking price."

"You say these things were worth a lot of money?" I asked.

"Heaps of money!" he affirmed. "The ruby, I dare say you know, is the most precious of all the great stones. The true ruby, the Oriental one, is found in greatest quantity in Burma and Siam, and the best are those that come from Mogok, which is a district lying northward of Mandalay. That's where these particular rubies originated—the ones the Quicks had lain their hands on. Moreover, I know how and where those villains took possession of them."

"Yes?" I said, feeling that another dark story lay behind this declaration. "Not honestly, I suppose?"

"Far from it!" he replied with a grim smile. "Those two rubies formed the eyes of some ugly god in a heathen temple in the Kwang-Tung province of Southern China. The Quicks gouged them out—according to their own story—then cleared off sharpish after that."

"You saw the rubies?" I asked.

"More than once," Baxter nodded, "on that island in the Yellow Sea. Noah and Salter would have bartered both for a ship at one time. But you may lay your life that when they boarded that Chinese fishing-boat, they paid for their passage as meanly as possible. No, my belief is that they still had those rubies on them when they turned up in England again, as likely as not. Take all the circumstances of the murders into consideration—in each case the dead man's clothing was ripped to pieces, the linings examined, even the padding at chest and shoulder torn and scattered. What were the murderers seeking for? Not for money—as far as I remember, each man had a good deal of money on him, and not a penny was touched. My own belief is that after Salter Quick joined Noah at Devonport, both brothers were steadily watched by men who knew what they had on them, and that when Salter came North he was followed, just as Noah was tracked down at Saltash."

I felt that here, in this lonely cove, we were a good deal nearer the solution of the mystery that had baffled Scarterfield, ourselves, the police, and everybody else. So apparently did Miss Raven, who suddenly turned to our curious host.

"Mr. Baxter," she said, colouring a little at her own temerity. "Why don't you follow Mr. Middlebrook's advice—give up the old silver to the authorities and help them track down the real murderers? Wouldn't that be better than stealing away?"

Baxter laughed, flung away his cigar, then rose to his feet smartly.

"A deal better from many standpoints, my dear young lady!" he exclaimed. "But it's too late for Netherfield Baxter to do anything 'cept follow his own coarser instincts."

"You'll get caught, you know," I said, as good-humouredly as possible. "You'll never get this stuff across the Atlantic and into a Yankee port without detection. As you are treating us well, your secret's safe enough with us—but think, man, of the difficulties of taking your loot across an ocean! To say nothing of Customs officers on the other side."

"I never said we were going to take it across the Atlantic," he answered coolly and with another of his cynical laughs. "I said we were going to sail this bit of a craft across—and so we are— but when we strike New York or Buenos Aires, the stuff won't be there."

"You mean you have a buyer close at hand?" I asked, after pondering the meaning of his statement.

Baxter offered an enigmatic smile. "The door of its market is yawning for it, Middlebrook, and not far away. If this craft drops in at Aberdeen, and the Customs folks come aboard, they'll find nothing but three innocent gentlemen, and their servants, a-yachting it across the free seas. Anyway, it's getting late—I'll send Chuh in with hot water. If you want anything more, feel free to ask it of him. As for me, I shan't see you again tonight—I must keep a watch for my pal coming aboard from his little mission ashore."

Then, with curt politeness, he bade us both good night, and went off on deck, and we two captives looked at each other.

"What a decidedly strange man!" murmured Miss Raven.

"That is no exaggeration," I conceded.

"And yet I feel sure he means us no harm. What do you think?"

"The same," I said, "but I'm still going to mount guard here and keep a night-time vigil. If I should have occasion to call you, for any reason, please do as I ask."

"Of course," she said, smiling appreciatively.

The Chinaman, who'd been in evidence at intervals, came into the little saloon with a can of hot water and disappeared into the cabin which had been given up to Miss Raven. She softly said good-night to me, reassured by my stated plan, then followed him inside. I heard her talking to this strange makeshift for a maid for a moment or two; then the man came outside while she closed and fastened the door on him. He then turned to me, asking in a soft voice if there was anything I pleased to need.

"Nothing but the rugs and pillows that your master spoke of," I answered.

He bent down and opened a locker to his right, producing a number of cushions and blankets, before making up a very tolerable couch for me. Then, he too departed, with a polite bow, and I was left alone with my thoughts.

Of one thing I was firmly determined—I was not going to allow myself to sleep that night. I firmly believed in Baxter's good intentions—in spite of his shady record, there was something in him that won one's confidence. He was unprincipled, without doubt, and the sort of man who would be all the worse if resisted, but at the time he seemed to evidence a certain pride in showing people like ourselves that he could behave himself like a gentleman. That said, he was only one amongst a crowd. For all I knew, his French friend might be as consummate a villain as ever walked the earth, and the Chinese cut-throats of the best quality. And there, behind a mere partition, was a helpless young woman who I had grown immensely fond of. It was a highly serious and unpleasant situation, at the best of it, and the only thing I could do was to keep awake and remain on the alert until morning came.

I took off coat and waistcoat, folded a blanket shawl-wise around my shoulders, wrapped another round my legs, and made myself fairly comfortable in the cushions which the Chinaman had deftly arranged in an angle of the cabin. I had directed him to settle my night's quarters in a corner close to Miss Raven's door, facing the half-dozen steps which led upwards to the yacht's deck. At the head of those steps was a door, which I'd asked him to leave open, so that I might have plenty of air.

When he'd gone, I extinguished the lamp which swung from the roof and faced the patch of sky framed in the open doorway. Half-sitting, half-lying amongst my cushions and rugs, I saw that the night was a clear one and that the heavens were full of glittering stars. After refilling and lighting my pipe, I lay there for a long time, smoking and thinking. My thoughts were somewhat confused, ranging over a motley array of subjects, many of which still continued to trouble me. The whirl of it all made me more than once feel disposed to sleep and I realized that, in spite of everything, I should struggle to stay awake all night.

Everything on board that strange craft was as still as the skies above her decks. I heard no sound whatever, save a very gentle lapping of the water against the vessel's timbers, and the occasional far-off hooting of owls in the woods that overhung the cove. I had to keep smoking to prevent myself from dropping into a doze, and two or so hours must have passed in that fashion. It was therefore midnight—or a little thereafter—when I heard the plashing of oars off in the distance, and snapped awake.

This, I surmised, was the Frenchman, coming back from his latest clandestine mission. Somehow—I could not well account for it—the mere fact of his return made me nervous and uneasy. On Baxter's own showing, the Frenchman had been hanging about that coast for some little time, just as Salter Quick descended upon it. And like Baxter, if Baxter's story were true, he was aware that one or other of the Quicks carried those valuable rubies. Even if the York alibi could be taken at face value, he might be privy to the doings of some accomplice who had carried out the killing. Either way, he was a doubtful quantity, and the mere fact that he was back again on that yawl made me more resolved than ever to keep awake.

I heard the boat come alongside. Then steps on deck, just outside my open door. Followed by the sound of Baxter's voice. Presently, too, I heard other voices—one belonging to the Frenchman, which I recognised from having heard him speak that afternoon. The other: a soft, gentle, amused-sounding voice was undoubtedly that of another foreigner. It seemed probable that it belonged to the Chinese gentleman of whom I had heard so much.

So now the three principal actors in this affair were all gathered together, separated from me and Miss Raven by a few planks, and close by were three more Chinese of whose qualities I knew nothing. Safe we might be—if Baxter was as good as his word—but we were certainly on the very edge of a hornet's nest.

I heard the three men talking together in low, subdued tones for a few minutes. Then they went along the deck above me and the sound of their steps ceased again. But as I lay there in the darkness, two round discs of light suddenly appeared on a mirror which hung from the cabin wall, and I saw that in the bulkhead behind me there were two similar holes, pierced in what was probably a door.

Behind that, under a newly-lighted lamp, the three men were now certainly gathered.

I was desperately anxious to know what they were doing— anxious to the point of nervousness— and would have given much to hear even a few words of their conversation. After a time of miserable indecision—for I was afraid of doing anything that would lead to suspicion or resentment on their part—I determined to look through the holes in the door and see whatever was to be seen.

I got out of my wrappings so noiselessly that I don't believe anyone else would have heard even a rustle. Tip-toeing in my stockinged feet across to the bulkhead, I put an eye to one of the keyholes. To my great joy, I found that I could see into the place to which Baxter and his companions had retreated. It was a sort of cabin, rougher in accommodation than that in which I stood, fitted with bunks on three sides, and furnished with a table in the centre. The three men stood round this table, examining some papers. A lamp hung directly overhead, shining its light on all three.

Baxter stood there in his shirt and trousers, as did the Frenchman, but the third man was dressed most splendidly. A small, sleek Chinaman, he wore a velvet-collared overcoat thrown open to reveal a smart dark tweed suit, and an elegant gold watch-chain festooned across the waistcoat. He was smoking a cigar of the finest quality, as I could tell from the aroma that floated toward me. And on the table before the three stood a whisky bottle, a syphon of mineral water, and glasses, which had evidently just been filled.

Baxter and the Frenchman stood elbow to elbow. The Frenchman held in his hands a number of sheets of paper, foolscap size, the contents of which he was obviously drawing to Baxter's attention. Presently they turned to a desk which stood in one corner of the place, where Baxter, lifting its lid, produced a big ledger-like book over which they bent, comparing certain entries with the papers in the Frenchman's hand. What book or papers they might be, I knew nothing, for all of this was done in silence.

It was then my attention was dragged away by a covert drama that was playing out behind them. A sight that turned me almost sick with a nameless fear and set me trembling from head to toe.

The dapper Chinaman, immovable save for an occasional puff of his cigar, stood silently on one side of the table as the two men bent over the corner desk. But then like a flash, his long, thin fingers went into a waistcoat pocket and with lightning-fast dexterity, he dropped something small and white—some tabloid or pellet— into two of the glasses on the table, which sank and dissolved with no less haste.

A moment or two later, Baxter and the Frenchman turned

round again after storing the ledger-like book inside the desk, along with the papers. By which time their companion was placidly smoking his cigar and sipping the contents of his own glass between idle puffs.

I was by that time desperately careless as to whether I might or might not be under observation. I remained where I was, my eye glued to that ventilation-hole, watching the menacing scene play out. For it seemed to me that the Chinaman was purposely drugging his companions for some unknown and insidious purpose. For one moment I was half-minded to rush round to the other cabin and tell Baxter what I had just seen—but I reflected that I might possibly bring about an affair of bloodshed, and perhaps murder. For if this Chinese was in league with his countrymen, the four of them might be inclined to dispense with subtlety and let blunt violence carry the day. No—the only thing to do was to wait, and wait I did, with a thumping heart and nerves tingling.

Baxter gulped down his drink at a single draught. The Frenchman took his in two leisurely swallows, then each flung himself on his bunk, pulled his blankets about him, and, as far as I could tell, seemed to fall asleep instantly. The Chinaman, as expected, was more deliberate and punctilious. He took his time over his cigar and whisky before pulling out a suitcase from some nook or other and producing from it a truly gorgeous sleeping-suit of gaily-striped silk. It occupied him quite twenty minutes to get undressed and into his grandeur, and even then he lingered, carefully folding and arranging his daytime garments. In the course of this, and in moving about the narrow cabin, he took casual glances at Baxter and the Frenchman, and I saw from his satisfied smile that each was sound asleep. Finally, he thrust his feet into a pair of bedroom slippers, as loud in their colouring as his pyjamas, and turned down the lamp with a twist of his fingers before gliding out of the door into the darkness above.

❈ 25 ❈

Now I heard steps, soft as snowflakes, go along the deck above me. For an instant they paused by the open door at the head of my stairway, then went on again, and all was silent as before. But in that silence, above the gentle lapping of the water against the side of the yawl, I heard the furious thumping of my own heart (and I did not wonder at it, nor was I ashamed of the fear that made it start so). Clearly, whatever else it might mean, if Baxter and the Frenchman were soundly drugged, Miss Raven and I were at the mercy of a pack of adventurers.

The Chinese gentleman in the flamboyant pyjamas had, without doubt, repaired to his compatriots in the galley, where they were no doubt sunk in conference. Were they going to murder Baxter and the Frenchman for the sake of the swag now safely on board? It was possible. I had heard many a tale far less so. No doubt this mysterious stranger was a man of subtlety and craft, as too was Lo Chuh Fen, based on Baxter's account of him. And if Wing was one of the other two, as Miss Raven had confidently surmised, then there would be brains enough for the carrying out of any nefarious plot.

It seemed to me as I stood there in something of a panic—a

peace-loving gentleman of bookish tastes, who scarcely knew one end of a revolver from the other—that the Chinese were going to round on their English and French associates, collar the loot for themselves, and sail the yawl—Heaven alone knew where! But in that case, what was going to become of me and my equally helpless companion? It hardly seemed likely that these mutineers would treat us with the same consideration as Netherfield Baxter, who—it now struck me—was an appealing combination of Dick Turpin and Don Quixote.

An hour passed. It may have been more; it may have been less; I cannot say with any certainty. All the while I felt like an accused man waiting in a cell on a jury's deliberations. Once or twice I thought of daring everything, rousing Miss Raven, and attempting an escape by means of the boat which lay at the side of the yawl. But reflection suggested that so desperate a deed would only mean getting a bullet through me, and perhaps through her as well. Then I speculated on my chances of toptoeing to the hatch of the galley, with the idea of listening. Again, reflection warned me that such an adventure would as likely as not end up with a few inches of cold steel in my side or through my gullet.

It was then, with my anxieties sharply in the ascendant, I turned around to see a man stood barely ten feet away. Without a sound—or none that I'd detected—he'd descended the stairs leading to the deck and moved within striking distance, or as near as. Seriously panicked, I was on the point of making a frenzied leap across the intervening space when Lo Chuh Fen held up one hand in a calming gesture and spoke in a low voice.

"Can you row a boat?"

I shall never forget that scarcely perceptible whisper, putting paid to my worst fears. At first, I merely nodded, unable to get the words out, but then I managed a single, strangled articulation: "Yes."

He pointed to the door behind which lay Miss Raven.

"Wake missie, as quietly as possible," he whispered. "Tell her get ready—come on deck—make no noise. All ready for you—then you go ashore and away, see? Not good for you to be here longer."

"No danger to her?" I asked him.

"No danger to anybody, you do as I say," Lo Chuh Fen answered.

Without another word, he turned and glided back up the stairway. For a few seconds I stood there, racked with indecision. Was it a trick? Should we be safe on deck or a target for flashing knives and bullets? But what was the alternative? To simply stay put? That course of action seemed even more hopeless and doom-laden.

Making up my mind, I turned around and gave the gentlest of raps on the door to Miss Raven's small cabin. Several seconds later, it opened a crack.

"Yes?"she whispered blearily, still rising from sleep.

"You must dress at once and come out," I said, trying to express as much urgency as I could without raising my voice in the slightest.

"I've never been undressed," she answered. "I lay down in my clothes."

Good," I said. "Then follow me up on deck. We're leaving."

Despite her quizzical frown, Miss Raven was out of the room at once and standing next to me.

"Don't be afraid," I whispered.

"Leaving?" she said, still trying to make sense of my injunction.

Nodding vigorously, I began to lead the way.

I went before her up the stairway and out onto the open deck. The night was particularly clear; the stars very bright; the patch of water between the yawl and shore perfectly calm by all appearances. We could see the woods above the cove quite plainly, and, at the edge of them, a ribbon of silver-sanded beach. Also, at the forward part of the vessel, I fancied I saw several shadowy forms. But before I could make any effort to distinguish them, Lo Chuh Fen reappeared to our right.

Without a word, he motioned for us to follow, preceded us along the side of the yawl to the boat, went before us into it, helped us down, put the oars into my hands, then climbed out again.

"Pull straight ahead," he said. "Good landing place straight before you: dry place on beach. Morning come soon; you get away through woods."

"The boat?" I asked him.

"You leave boat there. Anywhere," he answered. "Boat not wanted again—we go soon as high water over bar."

"Bless you!" I said. Then, remembering that I had three or four loose sovereigns in my pocket, I thrust a hand therein, pulled them out, and forced them into the man's hands. I heard Lo Chuh Fen chuckle softly before his head disappeared behind the rail of the yawl. Then, without further ceremony, I shoved the boat off.

For the next few minutes, I bent to those oars as I had never bent to any labour in my life, mental or physical. Miss Raven, seeing my earnestness, quietly took the tiller and steered us in a straight line for the spot which Lo Chuh Fen had indicated. Neither of us—strange as it may seem—spoke a single word until, at the end of half an hour's steady pull, the boat's front end ran on to the shingly beach beneath a fringe of dwarf oak that came right down to the edge of the shore.

I sprang from the vessel with a feeling of immense gratitude, impossible to describe in all of its richness. Between us, the boat being a light one, we managed to pull it across the pebbles and under the low cliff beneath the overhanging fringe of woodland. In the uncertain light—for since our setting out, masses of cloud had come up from the south-east—the old forest looked impenetrably black.

"We shall have to wait here until the dawn comes," I remarked. "We can't find our way through the wood in this darkness—I can't even recollect the path, if there was one, by which they brought us down from the ruins. You had better sit in the boat and make yourself comfortable with those rugs that Lo Chuh Fen provided."

Miss Raven got into the boat again, wrapped one rug round her knees, and placed another about her shoulders.

"What does all this mean?!" she asked passionately. "Why have they let us go? Can you tell me that?"

"No idea," I answered. "But a good many things have happened since Baxter said goodnight to us . . ." And I went on to tell her of all that had taken place since she'd retired to her cabin. "It seems very likely," I said in summation, "that the Chinese intend foul play for those two."

"Do you mean that they intend to murder them?" she asked, clearly distressed by the speculation.

"As like as not," I acknowledged. "It seems to me that a man who's lived the life of Netherfield Baxter might expect to meet with such a violent end. And I dare say the same is true of his French friend as well."

"Horrible," she murmured, drawing the blankets closer about her.

I nodded in agreement, then sought to put my grisly forecast in perspective. "As for ourselves, we're most uncommonly lucky to have avoided the same fate."

Staring back out to sea, Miss Raven adopted more of a pensive look. "But surely those men must know that, once free of them, we would be sure to give the alarm? We weren't under any promise to them as we were to Baxter."

"I don't understand anything," I said. "All I know is the surface of the situation. But that gentle villain who saw us off the yawl said that they were sailing at high water—only waiting until the tide was deep on the bar. And they could get a long way, north or south or east, before we could set anybody on to them. Supposing they did get rid of Baxter and his Frenchman, what's to prevent them making off across the North Sea to some far flung Russian port? They've got stuff on board that yacht that would be saleable anywhere."

Once more she was silent, but when Miss Raven spoke again, it was with evident conviction.

"No, I don't think that's it. They're dependent on wind and weather. Chances are they'd still be caught on our information—the seas aren't as wide as all that."

"What is it, then?" I asked.

"Supposing the Chinese plan to hand over Baxter and the Frenchman to the police, along with their plunder? We thought Wing was on board. If so, I think I may be right in offering such a suggestion. Supposing that he came across these people when he went to London; took service with them in the hope of getting at their secret; and induced the other Chinese to participate in his covert planning. In short, he's been playing the part of detective. Wouldn't that explain why they sent us away?"

"Partly yes; perhaps wholly," I said, struggling with this new idea. "But where do they intend to do the handing over if your theory's correct?"

"That's easy enough," she replied quickly. "There's nothing to do but sail the yawl into Berwick harbour and call the police aboard."

"I wonder if it's so?" I answered, musingly. "If we stay here until it's light, and the tide's up, we can see which way the yawl goes."

"I think I'm more inclined to head homewards at the earliest opportunity," said Miss Raven. "Mightn't we follow the coastline while the tide is still out?"

"I'm doubtful about our ability to get round the south point of this cove," I answered. "I was looking at it yesterday afternoon from the deck of the yawl, and a sheer wall of rock runs right out into the sea."

"Then, the woods," she said. "Surely we can make our way through them somehow? Dawn is nearly upon us and it'll soon enough be light."

"If you'd like to try it," I answered. "But it's darker in there than you think, and rougher going, I imagine."

Before she could reply, a clear and unmistakable sound carried across the water. It was a revolver shot, followed almost instantly by another one, three-quarters of a mile away. Miss Raven rose to her feet as a third shot rang out, followed by a fourth and then a fifth. With each firing, we saw bright flashes emanating from the *Blanchflower's* deck.

Half a dozen reports rang out in quick succession. Then another two or three, all mingling together. After that, as suddenly as they'd started up, the sounds and flashes died out. A heavy silence followed, which we both succumbed to, staring at the black bulk lying motionless on the grey water. During the furious melee, a faint yellow luminescence had risen above the far horizon. By the light of it, we could now see another craft off to our right, tearing along at breakneck speed, somewhere outside the sandbar, but still close to shore.

❧ 26 ❧

As we stood there transfixed, the sky seemed to lighten again while this low-lying hulk of a vessel shot around the cove's southern edge. It was coming along about half a mile outside the bar, at a rare turn of speed which would, I knew, quickly carry it beyond our field of vision. I was wondering whether it would continue on its way, full steam ahead, when the craft began to describe a great circle, coming slowly towards the bar, nosing about the *Blanchflower* like a terrier at the lip of some rat-hole.

Up to that moment, Miss Raven and I had kept silent throughout the ensuing drama, but now she turned to me and sought clarification.

"It's a gunboat or something of that sort, isn't it?"

"Torpedo-destroyer," I answered in the affirmative. "And the latest class, too."

"Wicked-looking things, aren't they? Although it looks as if it can't get over that sandbar as yet."

"The tide's rising fast, though," I remarked, pointing to the shore immediately before us.

To gain a better vantage point, we retreated further up the beach, amongst the overhanging trees, and then looked seaward again from beneath the shelter of a group of dwarf oaks. The destroyer lay supine outside the sandbar, watching its prey intently. Suddenly, right behind her, the sun shot up above the horizon and her long dark hull cut across its ruddy face. By its light, we were able to make out shapes that moved here and there on deck. As for the yawl, which was no less illumined, there were no visible signs of life.

Yet, even as we stared at the *Blanchflower,* off in the distance, a shot rang out again, followed by two others in sharp succession. Wondering what this new affray could be, we saw a smaller boat shoot out from beneath its bows, with a low, crouching figure inside of it. However, somebody onboard the yawl was just as eager to prevent the escape as the fugitive was to make it. Another three or four shots sounded—and at the last of these, the figure in the boat fell forward with a sickening suddenness.

"They got him!" I said. "The poor devil!"

"No!" exclaimed Miss Raven. "See!—he's up again."

The figure was struggling to an erect position—even at that distance we could make out the effort—but the light of the newly-risen sun was so dazzling that we could not discern the man's identity. Whoever he was, he managed to rise to his feet and lift an arm in the direction of the yawl, from which he was then some twenty yards away, and let off a shot with his own pistol. Two more shots rang out, returning fire, but neither hit its mark, and the escapee was busy at his oars now. Then the gunfire ceased as the boat drew further away from immediate danger in the direction of a spit of land some three hundred yards from where we stood. There were high rocks at the sea end of that spit—the boat disappeared behind them.

"There's one villain loose, at any rate," I muttered, not well pleased to think that he was within easy reach of ourselves. "Although I'm sure he was winged—he fell in a heap—and I dare say he'll take to the woods if he's still able."

"Look!" cried Miss Raven. "That naval vessel has sent out a smaller boat."

Following her pointing hand, I watched its crew of blue-jackets rowing manfully, traversing the sandbar, making directly for the *Blanchflower*.

"They're going to board her," I said. "I wonder what they'll find?"

"Dead men," answered Miss Raven, quietly.

I gave a sombre nod. "After all that shooting, it seems likely that at least one poor soul has lost his life today."

Miss Raven offered another sharp exclamation, and pointed again, this time towards the scene of the gun battle. From the yawl's forecastle, a black column of smoke suddenly shot up, followed by a great lick of flame.

"Good heavens!" I exclaimed. "It's on fire!"

By that time, the boat's crew from the destroyer had crossed the bar, entered the cove, and their vigorously impelled oars were flashing fast in the sheltered waters. The boat disappeared behind the drifting smoke that poured out from the yawl, then presently we saw figures hurrying hither and thither on the flaming deck.

Although deeply absorbed by these shocking events, a sudden movement away to my right, back on dry land, claimed my full attention. On the strip of pebble beneath the woods, a group of figures had just rounded the extreme point of the cove at its southernmost confines. There were several figures in the group, two of them mounted, and presently these two riders hastened towards us.

"The cavalry!" I exclaimed. "Look, that's Mr. Raven in front, and surely that's Lorrimore behind him!"

Miss Raven gazed at the approaching figures, shielding her eyes from the glare of the mounting sun, then ran forward along the shingle to meet them. By the time I'd caught her up, Mr. Raven and Lorrimore were off their horses, the other members of the party had drawn level, and my beleaguered companion was already relating events, summing it all up in an admirably concise fashions. Her uncle listened with simple, open-mouthed astonishment. Lorrimore, when mention was made of the Chinese element, attended on her words with growing concern. He turned to me as Miss Raven finished.

"How many Chinese do you reckon were onboard?" he asked.

"Four—including the last arrival," I answered.

"And two English?" he inquired.

"One Englishman, and one Frenchman," said I. "My belief is that the Chinese have settled these two—and then possibly split into separate factions. There's one man still at large in these woods, as Miss Raven explained. Whether he's a Chinaman or not, it's impossible to say."

He stared at me wonderingly for a moment; then turned and looked at the yawl. Evidently the blue-jackets had succeeded in checking the fire onboard. The flames had died down, and the smoke hung in wreaths above the vessel. We could see several figures running actively about the deck.

"There may be men on there that need medical assistance," said Lorrimore. "Where's this boat you mentioned, Middlebrook? I'm going off to that vessel. Can two of you help pull me across there?"

"I'll go with you," said I. "The boat's just along here."

The search party was a mixed lot—a couple of local policemen, some gamekeepers, two or three fishermen, and one of Mr. Raven's men-servants. Two of the fishermen ran the boat into the water. Lorrimore and I sprang in.

"This is the most astonishing affair I ever heard of!" he said as he sat down at my side in the stern. "And according to Miss Raven, you actually suspect my man Wing to be onboard?"

Seeing his obvious worry, I strove to answer diplomatically. "Yes," I said. "The plum cake pointed to that. But there's no knowing for sure."

"You were probably safer than you knew, if he *was* close to hand," retorted Lorrimore.

"That may be so," I said. "But tell me—how did you and your posse come this way? Didn't Mr. Raven get a wire last night?"

"He did," came the reply, "but he'd already become anxious prior to receiving it, and had sent out some of his menfolk along the moors and cliffs in search of you. One of them, very late in the evening, came across a man who'd been cutting wood somewhere hereabouts and had seen you and Miss Raven close to shore in the company of two strangers. Mr. Raven's man returned close to midnight, and with this news, the old gentleman was thrown into a great state of alarm. He roused the whole community, including me, and we set off to find you."

"Well, it's a great relief to be among friends again," I answered.

Nodding distractedly, Lorrimore stared off at the *Blanchflower.* "I'm inclined to side with Miss Raven's opinion. I think that Wing may have been onboard this vessel, and it was thanks to him you got away."

"You've heard nothing of him since London?" I asked.

The doctor shook his head grimly. "Which is precisely why I feel he's been playing some deep game after coming into contact with these people."

We were now close to the yawl, gazing expectantly at the figures on deck. Two of these detached themselves from the rest, came to the side, and looked down on us. One was a grimy-faced young naval officer, very much alive to his job. The other, not quite so smoke-blackened, turned out to be Scarterfield.

"Good Heavens!" I muttered. "Look who it is!"

As we pulled up to the side of the yawl, he was evidently telling the young officer exactly who we were. Then, as we prepared to clamber aboard, the police detective addressed us without ceremony, as if we'd been parted from him for no more than a few minutes.

"You'd better be prepared for some unpleasant sights," he said. "This is no place to bring an empty stomach at this hour of the morning. And I fancy you've no great liking for horrors, Mr. Middlebrook?"

"I've had plenty of them during the night," said I. "I was a prisoner onboard this vessel from yesterday afternoon until the early morning hours. And I've sat on yonder beach watching a good many things that have gone on since."

Scarterfield stared at me in astonishment, as did his companion. "I don't understand it at all. You say you were on this vessel during the night? Then in God's name, who else was on her?"

"We left six men to the best of my knowledge. Netherfield Baxter, a Frenchman, a Chinese gentleman, and three more of his compatriots. The Frenchman and the Chinese gent were those fellows we heard of at Hull. And one of the others was Lo Chuh Fen, who needs no introduction."

"And you got into their hands—how?" he asked.

"Kidnapped—Miss Raven and myself—by Baxter and the Frenchman,," I answered. "We came across them by accident in those woods, yesterday afternoon, at the place where they'd just dug up the monastic silver. "

Seeing the chests a few yards to my right, I pointed them out to the detective.

Scarterfield threw a quick, disinterested glance at the ancient treasure, then turned his attention back to me. "Then one of them must have followed your lead and escaped from the vessel. There's only five persons safely accounted for—and every man Jack of them is dead!"

"One did escape," said I. "He got off in a boat just as you were approaching the bar yonder. I fancied that you'd seen him."

"No," he answered, shaking his head. "We didn't see anybody leave. The yawl lay between us and him most likely. Where did he land, do you know?"

"Behind that spit," I replied, pointing to the place. "He vanished beyond those black rocks. That was the last I saw of him. But he can't have got far, for he was certainly wounded—another man fired at him as he made his desperate escape."

"We heard those shots," said the lieutenant, "and we found a grievously wounded Englishman in the bows when we boarded.

The others were already dead by then, and this poor blighter joined them the minute after that."

"Not a man alive!" I exclaimed.

Scarterfield shook his head gravely. "Too late for your ministrations, Doctor Lorrimore."

Having been busy getting the fire under control, the bluejackets had up to then left the dead men where they found them —with one exception. The man whom they had found in the bows had been carried aft and laid near the entrance to the little deck-house, a white sheet thrown over him.

Lorrimore stepped toward it, and lifted the sheet up, revealing the bullet-riddled corpse of Netherfield Baxter.

"That's the fellow we found right forward," said the lieutenant. "He's several slighter wounds on him, but he'd been shot through the chest just before we boarded. That would be the shot fired by the man in the boat, I'm guessing. Either way, they must have had a most desperate do of it. This yawl looks like a bloody slaughterhouse!"

He was right there, and I was deeply thankful that Miss Raven and I had been sent ashore before the carnage began in earnest.

As Lorrimore went about, surveying the dead, I followed after him, despite my pronounced queasiness. As if to distract myself from the grisly spectacle, I endeavoured to form some idea, more or less accurate, of final events onboard the *Blanchflower*. It seemed to me that either Baxter or the Frenchman, awaking from sleep sooner than the Chinese had expected, had discovered that treachery was afoot, leading to a wholesale shoot-out. Most of the slaughter had taken place immediately in front of the hatchway which led to the cabin where I had seen Baxter and his two principal associates conferring. Some sort of a rough barricade had been hastily set up there, behind which the Frenchman lay dead. Before it, here and there on the deck, lay three of the Chinese, including their presumed leader, still in his gaily-coloured sleeping suit, although it was now pockmarked with bullet holes. Lo Chuh Fen was a little further away, fallen on his side, a pool of sticky blood surrounding him. The third man was lying on his back, near the wheel, his lifeless gaze aimed up at the morning heavens. All in all, it made for the most gruesome spectacle I had ever witnessed in my life.

27

S carterfield came and stood at my elbow as I stood
surveying these unholy sights.

"That fourth Chinaman," he said. "I must get hold of
him, dead or alive. The rest's nothing without him."

I glanced around. Lorrimore, after an inspection of the dead
men, had walked aside with the lieutenant and was in close
conversation with him.

"Scarterfield," I said in a whisper, "I've grounds for believing
that the fourth Chinaman is Wing—Lorrimore's servant."

"What!" he exclaimed. "The man we saw at Ravensdene
Court?"

"Just so," said I. "The same one who went off to London
looking for Lo Chuh Fen. And I think that Wing not only
discovered his compatriot, but came aboard this vessel with him
as part of a crew which Baxter got together at Limehouse or
Poplar.."

"And as for Lo Chuh Fen himself?"

Performing a half turn, I pointed to the man's dead body.

Staring down at it for a time, the detective transferred his
attention to the mortal remains of Netherfield Baxter. "And

you're sure that man lying dead there is the Baxter we heard of at Blyth and traced to Hull?"

"Absolutely certain," I told him. "It would no doubt help if I gave you my own summary of what happened yesterday and today . . ."

I told Scarterfield, as concisely as I could, how Miss Raven and myself had fallen into Baxter's hands, what had happened to us onboard, and, at somewhat greater length, of Baxter's story of his own career as it related to the theft of the monastic treasure, his connection with the *Elizabeth Robinson,* and prior knowledge of the brothers Quick. Nor did I forget Baxter's theory about the rubies, at which Scarterfield pricked his ears and nodded volubly.

"Now there's something in that," he said with a regretful glance at the place where Baxter's dead body lay. "I only wish that fellow had been alive to tell us more. For he's right about those rubies—I can confirm the Quicks had two in their possession."

It was my turn to evince a degree of astonishment. "How do you know that?" I asked.

"I had occasion to interview a Hatton Garden diamond merchant at our London headquarters, not three days ago, who was newly returned from the continent. Having familiarized himself with the particulars of the case, courtesy of the newspapers, he felt sure that Salter Quick was identical with a man with whom he'd not so long ago discussed the value of certain stones in this fellow's possession. During the course of their interview, Quick had divulged the items themselves and the merchant had found himself staring at a dozen or so of the most magnificent pearls he'd ever set eyes on, and a couple of rubies which he knew to be priceless. The merchant had advised Quick to let him assume safe custody of these treasures so that he might show them to potential buyers and auction them to the highest bidder. Instead, Quick had made his excuses, folding up his canvas wrapping again, remarking that he had a train to catch.

Then he hastened off, assuring the merchant he would call in a week or so, on his return from the North of the country, but needless to say, he never did."

"Salter Quick," I agreed. "It stands to reason. This fully corroborates Baxter's story of the rubies. He may not have mentioned any pearls, but the brothers' persistent greed and cunning explains how they would end up with these to boot."

The detective nodded his head. "It certainly fits in with all we know of them."

I now began to make a few tentative mental connections, based on Scarterfield's disclosure, the foremost of which I felt compelled to share with him:

"I'm starting to think that Salter Quick's murder lies at the door of one of these Chinamen."

The detective offered a wry smile. "You're not alone in that conjecture, although I haven't as yet had the time to flesh it out."

This mention of time—and the detective's sore lack of it—put me in mind of his admirable industriousness and all that he'd accomplished in a few short weeks.

"Perhaps you could tell me how you came to make such a dramatic entrance and intercept the *Blanchflower* first thing today?" I asked him.

Scarterfield afforded himself a slight chuckle at the thought of his grand entrance. "I got wind of Baxter's yawl down Limehouse way—learning that she'd been spotted in the Thames, and that her owner had enlisted a small crew of Chinamen and gone away with them. Not long after, there was a confirmed sighting of her off the Norfolk coast, heading northwards. So then I petitioned the authorities, laying it on thick about sea piracy in British waters, which prompted just the response I was looking for. They sent this destroyer in search of Baxter, with me safely onboard her, and here we both are."

Before the detective could elaborate any further, he was approached by the naval lieutenant.

"My men have the fire completely beaten," he said to Scarterfield. "If you want to examine the whole vessel, you can do so safely now."

Thanking him, Scarterfield moved off, gesturing for me to join him, as Dr Lorrimore came forward and showed willing. Together, we began a thoroughgoing examination of the yawl in an earnest attempt to reconstruct the bloody tragedy. Despite the ongoing mystery, and dizzying number of deaths, there were now a good many things that we had not known twenty-four hours before. One, that the many affairs of Netherfield Baxter, however dubious, had nothing to do with the murders of Noah and Salter Quick. Another, that those murders had arisen from the brothers' possession of pearls and rubies which Salter had shown to the Hatton Garden diamond merchant. As for Lo Chuh Fen, he'd doubtless learned of the precious stones existence on that lonely island in the South China Sea. Then, drifting eventually to England, he must have discovered the whereabouts of the two brothers and found that the rubies were still in their possession. Reason enough to engineer a secret conspiracy, recruiting among his countrymen, in order to secure the valuables at any cost. He himself had probably tracked Salter to the lonely bit of shoreline near Ravensdene Court, while another of his associates had fallen upon Noah at Saltash.

Despite the seeming ease with which I formed this hypothesis, it was far from unassailable. There was still the question of how this had led to the attack of the Chinese on Baxter and the Frenchman. Nor did it account for the identity of the man who'd left the yawl's company and escaped to shore.

A loud exclamation from Scarterfield interrupted these thoughts and called me over. He was examining the body of Lo Chuh Fen, aided by one of the blue-jackets.

"Look here," he said. "This chap has been searched—he wore a body-belt that's been violently torn from him and hacked to pieces!"

"No doubt the work of the man who got away in the boat," said I. "He must have sought the pearls and rubies as well."

Scarterfield gave a pensive frown. "And you're certain he was wounded while fleeing?"

I nodded in the affirmative. "I saw him fall headlong; he then recovered himself and fired the shot which finished Baxter. Whatever his injuries are, he pulled himself together and managed to row as far as shore."

"Well, if he's wounded, he can't get far without attracting notice," declared Scarterfield. "Still, we must be after him presently. A more detailed inspection of the crime scene will have to wait, along with a full inventory of the treasure. But first let's have a quick look at the quarters these Chinamen occupied in case that turns up another telling clue."

The smoke from the fire—which seemed to have broken out in the forecastle, and been confined to it by the heroic efforts of the sailors—had now almost cleared away. We went forward to the galley, which the fire had not spread to, and which looked refreshingly spick and span after the scenes of bloody mayhem astern and in the cabin. The various pots and pans shone gaily in the sun's glittering light. Every utensil was in its place; evidently the galley's controlling spirit had been a meticulously careful person who hated dirt and disorder. And on a shelf near the stove was laid out what I took to be the things which the cook had destined for breakfast—a tempting one of kidneys, bacon, soles, and curried eggs.

From this I gathered that the presiding genius of the galley had no notion of the impending mutiny, and pointed out the same thing to Scarterfield.

"Just so" agreed the detective. "And you think this orderliness adds further weight to the idea that Wing was the cook in question?

I considered my answer carefully. "I do. Although I never once caught sight of him, it has to be said. This supposition is still based on the taste of a plum cake as much as anything."

"Well, I've known of worse clues," he answered with a wry smile. "Believe you me."

At that moment, Lorrimore poked his head into the galley, having concluded his own investigations. After a cursory glance at the kitchen surroundings, he let out a sharp cry, extending his arm to claim a black silk cap which hung from a peg above the cooking stove.

"That's Wing's!" he said in emphatic tones. "My man must have been here!"

28

The bit of head-gear which Lorrimore had taken down assumed a startling new significance. For a few moments, Scarterfield and I gazed at the object as if it might actually speak to us. Nevertheless, the detective, when he presently spoke, evinced a certain scepticism.

"That's the sort of cap that most Chinamen wear," he remarked. "It may have belonged to any one of them."

"No!" answered Lorrimore with emphatic assurance. "That's my man's. I saw him making it. He's as deft with his fingers at that sort of thing, as he is at cooking. And since this cap is his, and as he's not amongst the dead, he must be the one that Middlebrook saw escaping. And since he is that man, I know where he's heading next."

"Where?" asked Scarterfield.

"To my house!" said Lorrimore in a raised voice.

Scarterfield retained his doubts, demonstrating them freely: "I don't think that's likely, doctor. Presumably, he's got those jewels on him, and I should rather say his intention was to get on a train unobserved and lose himself in Newcastle. A Chinaman with valuables on him to the tune of eighty thousand pounds? Come now—he'll want away!"

"You don't know that he's any valuables of any sort on him," retorted Lorrimore. "That's all mere supposition. And I say again that if my man Wing was on this vessel—as I'm sure he was—his intentions were wholly honourable. He might have fallen in with this felonious bunch, but you could not count him as one of them."

For his part, Scarterfield elected not to reply. Apparently, his belief in Chinese virtue was not as great as the doctor's. "Well," he said. "I'm on his track, anyhow. And I propose to get away to the beach. There's nothing more we can do here. These naval people have got this job in hand. Let's leave them to it."

As we made our way to the boat, three of the blue-jackets finally forced open the two wooden chests standing on deck. It was no easy business, for whether the dishonest bank-manager and Netherfield Baxter had ever opened them, they were screwed tight in a most conscientious fashion. But at last the lids were off—to reveal inner shells of lead; and within these, gleaming dully in the fresh sunlight, lay the much coveted monastic treasure.

Despite our haste, all three of us paused for a few moments and considered the massive bounty. At any other time, in a less fraught setting, I might have been able to admire these items objectively. But now they were inextricably linked with the terrible bloodshed onboard the *Blanchflower* and I could only think of them as accursed for that same reason.

Stopping next to the lieutenant, Scarterfield took from his pocket those parchments procured in Blyth and handed them to the naval officer. "Here is the list of what there ought to be. I don't know if it comes within the law of treasure trove, but I dare say the Crown solicitors will settle that point one way or another."

After boarding the boat, we rowed to shore without incident, and were joined by the rest of our party on disembarking, which now included two members of the local constabulary. As Scarterfield conferred with them, and Dr Lorrimore filled in Mr. Raven, I drew aside his niece.

"Don't be upset," I said, "but there wasn't a man alive onboard that vessel."

Miss Raven appeared to have braced herself for these grim tidings, and looked resigned for the most part.

"Baxter too?" she asked.

I nodded sombrely. "Wing alone avoided the common fate. He was the one we saw escaping."

"So it was as I thought—Wing was there?"

"Lorrimore is sure of it. He found his man's cap in the galley."

Detaching himself from the local police, Scarterfield came alongside us.

"We'd better get beyond these rocks while we're still able and see if we can pick up this fellow's scent."

Spreading ourselves out along the shore, we crossed the spit of sand as the tide started encroaching. Beyond the black rocks that jutted out of it, we came across the boat, still rocking in the lapping water. On the seat to the stern, and on one of the oars, blood was clearly visible.

A sharp cry from one of the men who had gone a little ahead of us brought the rest of the group over. Next to a shallow rock pool, there were marks in the sand, more evidence of blood, and strips of clothing—of linen or silk—as if the man had torn up his garments to staunch the bleeding.

"Probably washed his wounds here," observed Scarterfield; "aware that salt is a styptic. Flesh wounds most likely, although judging from what we've seen of the blood, he must have already been weakening by this point."

It was not difficult to discern a trail leading away from the pool, and we followed these erratic footprints across the sand, as far as the overhanging woods, where they merged into open moorland. There, in the short, wiry grass of the close-knitted turf, the marks promptly vanished.

"As I thought," muttered Lorrimore, striding on ahead. "He's made for my place just as I knew he would. There's a road at the head of these moors that runs parallel with the railway on one side and the coast on the other towards Ravensdene. Wing will have known this as the shortest route to strike the road and the village beyond it."

That the doctor was right, we were not long in finding out. Twice, as our party climbed the steep side of the moorland, we came across more evidence of the fugitive. On both occasions, he had sat down beneath trees, presumably to summon what little strength he was still able to drawn upon. At the second of these sites, we found another makeshift bandage that had been completely soaked through.

Seeing the stained fabric, Lorrimore shook his head, wearing an expression that combined amazement and anxiety. "No man could have got much further after losing so much blood."

Coming out on top of the moorland, and rounding the corner of the woods, we hit the road of which Lorrimore had spoken—a long, white ribbon of track that ran north and south through treeless country. There, a few yards away from us, stood an isolated cottage with a bit of unfenced garden before it. In that garden, a strange group had gathered as we were now able to see.

Mr. Cazalette was crouched with his back to us, although his figure was unmistakable. Standing next to him was the local police inspector, whose horse and trap were tethered close by. A woman and wide-eyed child stood off to one side, clearly unnerved by these strange happenings.

Drawing closer, we caught glimpses of towels and water and hastily-improvised bandages, and then the figure who Cazalette was ministering to. Wing was propped up against a bank of earth, his eyes closed, and over his face a queer grey-white pallor. His left arm and shoulder were bare, save for the fresh bandages which Cazalette was applying. The discarded ones lay nearby on the turf, soaked through with blood as before.

Lorrimore rushed forward with a hasty exclamation, and had

Cazalette's job out of the old gentleman's hands in seconds. As the wizened Scot stepped backward, retiring his services, he turned side-on to me.

"I think we were just about in time," he said, laconically. "I don't know what it all means, but I reckon the laddie was just about done for."

"You found him?" I asked.

"No. Yon woman was out in her garden, feeding her fowls, when she saw him stagger round the corner. Shortly after he fell across the bank in a dead faint, so she ran to fetch some water. Luckily, that was when me and the inspector happened by in the trap."

The police inspector himself now took a step forward.

"Fortunately, Mr. Cazalette was carrying a big flask of neat brandy with him, so we gave Wing a stiff dose which had something of a restorative effect. Mr. Cazalette says he's only incurred flesh wounds, but I don't know: the man's fainted twice since we got here. The last time, before he lost consciousness, he fumbled amongst his clothing, pulled something out. and shoved it into my hand as a matter of urgency. 'Give it Lorrimore,' he said, in a very weak voice. 'Tell him I found it all out—was going to trap them—but they were too quick for me.'

Still marvelling at this delirious statement, the inspector drew out a piece of plain canvas, all twisted up, and opened it before our wondering eyes. Inside were a heap of magnificent pearls and a couple of wonderful rubies that shone in the sunlight like fire.

"That's what he gave me," said the inspector, stunned by his receipt of them. "Now what do you make of that?"

"You're looking at the principle cause of Salter Quick's murder," said I. "And it's claimed more lives since, one way or another. I only hope that Wing here is spared the same fate."

❧ 29 ❧

After Lorrimore had patched up his faithful servant, and afforded him plenty of bed rest, we were invited to visit the brave invalid. In an armchair in the sitting room, with a blanket over his lap, Wing looked much recovered after a week's respite – a testament to his innate good health and the ministrations of the loyal doctor. It was a strange story he had to relate, although our narrator was matter-of-fact in the telling. He might have been explaining to us his recipe for plum cake instead of recounting a close brush with death.

As it turned out, after journeying to London at Scarterfield's behest, Wing had plunged into those quarters of the East End wherein his fellow-countrymen gather in number. His knowledge of the district, deep as he'd professed it to be, soon brought him in touch with Lo Chuh Fen. As Wing discovered, his compatriot had been in London for the last three years, assisting in the management of a Chinese eating-house. Taking lodgings nearby, Wing put himself up and renewed acquaintance with Chuh, who introduced him in turn to Ah Wong, a new associate.

There, before many days had passed, another Chinaman came on the scene—that suave associate of Netherfield Baxter's who I had seen for myself onboard *The Blanchflower.* Representing himself to Wing, Chuh, and Wong as the owner of a successful trading operation, he spoke of an Englishman and Frenchman who were shortly to make a crossing of the Atlantic in a small but well-appointed yacht. In light of this forthcoming voyage, he was offering all three of them gainful employment as crew members.

An introduction to Baxter and the Frenchman followed and the trio were promptly hired for the transatlantic journey. Moreover, they were taken into Baxter's confidence as regards the treasure hidden on the Northumberland coast, and a modest share of the proceeds was promised them on completion of the ocean crossing. One day later, the yawl left the Thames and headed northward. By this time, Wing had gained Chuh's confidence and learned that he was in possession of those pearls and rubies which Salter Quick had exhibited to the diamond merchant. Although Chuh was yet to confess to the robbery—or the murder attached to it—Wing was very much of the opinion that he'd committed both felonies, and that Ah Wong had been the one who'd dispatched Noah Quick at Saltash.

As the yawl sailed along the English coast, Wing improvised his own plans. By then, he'd discovered that its owners, after recovering the monastic treasures, were going to call at Leith, where they would be met by the private yacht of a wealthy American. Accordingly, he made up his mind to escape from the yawl on arrival, go straight to the police, and give them all the information they needed to execute not one, but two series of arrests.

Here Wing's plans were frustrated by the capture of myself and Miss Raven. Having learned of our kidnap, he was greatly concerned lest we should see him and conclude that he had joined the gang and become a party to its nefarious activities. However that same night, a far more serious development had materialized. Arriving from London to be met by the Frenchman at Berwick, the Chinese gentleman had made his fateful appearance.

Not one hour later, having drugged both principal associates, he'd unfolded his confident plans to his three fellow-country-men; proposing to get rid of the Europeans and seize the vessel and its contents for themselves, setting sail for a port in Northern Russia. Thinking on his feet, Wing had professed agreement—his only proviso being that Miss Raven and myself should be cleared out of the yawl in order to mitigate against the involvement of the British Navy. A proposition that was readily assented to, after which Chuh was charged with the job of sending us both ashore.

It was shortly afterwards that everything went awry with the conspirators' plans when the drug administered to Baxter and the Frenchman failed to produce the desired effect. Waking with a start as his would-be killers advanced on him, Baxter reached for his pistol and opened fire, waking his comrade in the process. A fierce gun battle ensued, during the course of which Wing barricaded himself into the galley.

When the shooting had finally stopped, he crept from it stealth-ily, surveying the bloody carnage, and came across Lo Chuh Fen's dead body. Stripping it of the belt which he knew to contain the precious stones, and a weapon still in his hand, Wing made for the boat which lay at the side of the yawl and hastily pushed off. It was then that Baxter, the only other survivor, sought to stymie his escape bid. Wing was hit below the ribs by the proceeding gunshot, but his return of fire did for the Northumbrian entirely. Weak and fainting after landing ashore, the Chinaman bound his wounds as best he was able and set out for his master's house, as we already knew.

So there it was—it only remained for the police to tie up any loose ends, and for Wing to be thoroughly exonerated for Baxter's death by misadventure. After these weeks of high drama, and serious jeopardy, this came as an enormous relief.

At dinner that night, back at Ravensdene Court, our party talked of little else, predictably. Nor was it unsurprising that Mr Cazalette should be the principle speaker and explainer-in-chief.

As wise after the event as he'd been before it, he put the whole thing in perspective for the rest of us. Indeed, such was the old Scot's enthusiasm for pontificating that he plain forgot his long-standing embargo on table talk. It was only when dessert was served that he quietened a little, allowing Mr. Raven the chance to speak.

The owner of Ravensdene Court turned promptly to me.

"Now that order has been restored, and peace with it, I trust you will continue with your inventory of my uncle's books and papers? I know that we have already detained you interminably, Mr Middlebrook, but I should be most obliged if you would see this task through."

It was a question that I had put to myself already as the dust started to settled on our murder mystery. Although I had not allocated a specific period of time to my stay in Northumberland, I'd expected to return to London long before summer. As I debated the matter again, I stole a glance at Miss Raven, who smiled at me across the table with what I perceived to be tacit encouragement.

After dinner, Messrs Cazalette and Raven retired to the study to further ruminate on Wing's testimony, while myself and Miss Raven begged an early night. As we climbed the stairs, side by side, a rare silence arose between us. It was only when we'd reached the door to her room that I sought to dispel it in a meaningful way, although I spoke with all the feigned casualness I could muster.

"Out of interest, would it please you if I stayed a little longer?"

Miss Raven paused before answering. "It wouldn't displease me," she said.

I smiled at her politic answer. "That still falls some way short of a fulsome endorsement."

She lifted her head and regarded me evenly. "And is my endorsement really of such value to you?"

Having been put on the spot, I saw no option except to divulge the truth of the matter.

"It's of immense value, Miss Raven. And the same can be said of your friendship. I would not be without it if I'm being honest."

I was glad that I had expressed myself so candidly, for it earned me the most radiant smile I had ever had the good fortune to elicit. There was a slight blush to Miss Raven's cheek, but her eyes were anything but evasive, and her expression was one of forthright affection.

"Then we are on the same page, Mr Middlebrook, I'm glad to say. Now let me bid you a good night."

THE END

Loveday Brooke, Lady Detective

A SECOND WIND CLASSIC
REISSUE

CATHERINE LOUISA PIRKIS

Move over, Sherlock...

By a jerk of Fortune's wheel, Loveday Brooke is thrown upon the world, penniless and all but friendless. Faced with disaster, she defies convention and chooses for herself a most unusual career.

Such is the starting premise for this remarkable collection of detective stories, showcasing Miss Brooke's astonishing powers of deduction and indomitable spirit in the face of rampant criminality and male scepticism alike.

Printed in Great Britain
by Amazon

38940332R00118